The Landmark Library
No. 10

DON TARQUINIO

The Landmark Library

OLIVER ONIONS
In Accordance with the Evidence
Widdershins

GEORGE MOORE
Celibate Lives

ARNOLD BENNETT
Mr. Prohack

T. F. POWYS
The Left Leg

MARGARET IRWIN
Still She Wished for Company

ANN BRIDGE
The Ginger Griffin

CHARLES MORGAN
The Gunroom

C. E. MONTAGUE
Rough Justice

FR. ROLFE
Don Tarquinio

DON TARQUINIO

A KATALEPTIC PHANTASMATIC ROMANCE

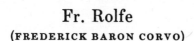

Fr. Rolfe
(FREDERICK BARON CORVO)

Neve me impedias
neve longius persequaris

ὅπως μήτε ἀντιστήσει μοι μήτε ἕψει
πορρωτέρω

CHATTO & WINDUS

LONDON

Published by
Chatto & Windus Ltd.
London
*
Clarke, Irwin & Co. Ltd.
Toronto

First published 1905
This edition first published in 1969

SBN 7011 1384 7

Printed in Great Britain
by William Lewis (Printers) Limited
Cardiff

TO
H. R.
FROM HIS
AFFECTIONATE
BROTHER

To some, Love comes so splendid and so soon,
　　With such wide wings, and steps so royally,
　　That they, like sleepers wakened suddenly
Expecting dawn, are blinded by His noon.

To some, Love comes so silently and late,
　　That all unheard He is ; and passes by,
　　Leaving no gift but a remembered sigh,
While they stand watching at another gate.

But some know Love at the enchanted hour :
　　They hear Him singing like a bird afar :
　　They see Him coming like a falling star :
They meet His eyes—and all their world's in flower.

ETHEL CLIFFORD

PROLOGUE

Dear Herbert:

When the last century was a-dying, a certain idiot asked me to write the history of one day in the life of a man of fashion in the era of the Borgia. It was to include every single act and deed of his during a given four-and-twenty hours : because it was wanted for a magazine, which proposed to publish a series of such histories illustrating the manners and customs of the Smart Set in all ages.

Of course I instantly thought of the holographs which Don Tarquinio Giorgio Drakontoletes Poplicola di Santacroce wrote for the edification of his son Prospero. They purport to have been written about 1523-1527, as the leisurely effort of a man of unbounded

energy very anxious to express himself; and
there was one of them which certainly seemed
pat to my purpose. It actually did describe
all Don Tarquinio's doings on one day in
1495, from (a little before) 6 p.m. to 6 p.m.
round the clock. It was very exciting and
very comical.

So I did it. But it was by no means easy:
as you'll readily understand when I hint
that the frightful man wrote an Italian jargon
of his own, which was all Greek where it
wasn't Latin. No doubt the fashion of his
age was to write macaronics: but consider
his English tralator's difficulties!

And then again, think what it means to
boil down a book into a magazine article.
You see, the terms of my commission were
that I was to set down everything the
gentleman did. But he did such a lot.
And he explained it all so voluminously,
with a wealth of detail which simply could
not be omitted.

And of course my version was rejected.

It was a mere category — not a story. I myself could see that.

I put the thing in a cupboard with curses, on the idiot who had invited me to do a useless thing, on myself for being ass enough to waste four months in trying to make a sow's ear out of a silken purse —I mean, in attempting to compress a piece of real and serious and elaborate history, and an amazingly amusing character study. and a breathlessly intricate story of adventure, into a merely ephemeral ten pages or so of journalism.

There the papers lay until a week ago, when I had just finished my new book, and was rummaging among my belongings with the idea of tidying-up before beginning something fresh.

They looked as though they might be interesting.

I took them out ; and conned them over.

Little by little I saw what an accented

fool I had been not to let Don Tarquinio
tell his own tale, in his own quaint acute
humorous sensuous conscientious way.   For
it's all nonsense to say that the Fifteenth
Century can't possibly speak to the Twentieth,
because it is the Fifteenth and not the
Twentieth, and because those two centuries
haven't got a Common Denominator.   They
have.   It's Human Nature.

And, so, since you're always bothering
me to write a book which is not about
silly Catholic clergymen, or incomprehensible
antiquities, or abnormal modernities—for once
I'll let my Waterman's Ideal be his Barnum,
and tralate to you Don Tarquinio's holograph.

You'll find him and his fellows just as
deliciously and comically silly, and just as
haphazardly and unexpectedly wise, and just
as good, and just as bad, as the people whom
you meet every day of your life, who always
go such a frightfully long way round in
their endeavours to attain their objects,—and
not a bit like the disagreeably unnatural

people in ordinary books who persistently do the right thing in the right way at the right moment.

In short, if you're interested in human beings, these are your ones.

Read what Tarquinio says of himself, and his plight and his longings. Mark how he tells the story of his fortunate day. Learn how he risked his life to win release from the Great Ban, anxious to act as a prince should, and to live, and to love.

From CRABS HERBOROUGH,
  On the Feast of Saint Mildred.

DON TARQUINIO

I

DURING the present year, the first of the
paparchy of Clement,[1] Messer Francesco
Guicciardini and Messer Paolo Giovio came
from Fiorenza, bringing to me their well-
written manuscripts : to the end that I might
read the same, and praise them or vituperate
them, as well for the purity of letters as for
the good of the race of men.

But the said manuscripts ought to be burned ;
and no copy of them ought to be preserved.
These scribes are, as I have said, of Fiorenza ;
and they have written of events which took
place in the City[2] when they were little boys.

---

[1] Pope Clement the Seventh began to reign
A.D. 1523.

[2] Rome is the only " City " to a Roman.

They have no means of knowing these events, except from hearsay. They have dared to write that which they have heard: for they certainly never saw. But we know well that it is impossible for any man of Fiorenza truthfully to intreat of Roman events, by cause of the hatred, indelible, Carthaginian, which all Fiorentini always bear to us Romans. And I myself do know these their histories to be false and shameful: for I indeed was concerned in the making of history here in the City, at the same time of which these men have dared to write mendaciously.

Messer Francesco is a rather vain vacuous man, incapable of dealing with grave matters. I believe that he wisheth to be honest: but his shallow mind causeth him to collect gossip, without testing its truth, as may be seen in the manuscript which he will not burn, where They say, and It is said, and I am told that, and other suchlike forms are reiterated.

Messer Paolo, on the other hand, hath written gossip as though it were history: nor hath he deemed it right to qualify his assertions in the manner of the aforesaid Messer Francesco. Moreover, when I plainly showed him how that, to mine own knowledge, certain of his allegations were false, he audaciously responded in these three words, saying:

"The people wish to be deceived. I will deceive them in return for gold sequins.[1] And, after an hundred years, my mendacity will have become verity."

The said Messer Paolo thus hath confessed himself to be a liar, flagrant, impenitent. So long as he was content to write of those things of which he had cognition, for example the Book About Fishes[2] which lately hath been printed, so long he was worthy of observance as a rather rustic pagan man who diligently used his little ability. But, seeing that he

---

[1] The gold zecchino was worth about half-a-guinea, but it had about four times the latter's purchasing value.

[2] I suppose Don Tarquinio to mean *De Piscibus Romanis*, published A.D. 1524.

B

not only hath written many falsehoods but also openly hath boasted of the same, let him and his dead be anathema.

It appeareth to me that the writing of history is a simple matter. Let each man, from the age of puberty, write of the things which happen to himself. So few men can write that not more than enough will be written. Also, some men, having been born under benignant stars, will rise : while others, having been born under malignant stars, will fall. The writings of the first will live; and their successors will profit by reading what they have written. The writings of the second die and disappear with the corruptible carcase of their writers.

Wherefore I myself will write the history of one day of mine own life, in order that thou, my son, mayst learn the true method of writing history : that is to say, with knowledge, with a share in the fact, with truth as before the priest, with accurate descriptions of persons and things, but chiefly without any desire of persuading. But the four stumbling-blocks to truth, which the Anglican mage[1] invented, must be avoided, and they are :

The influence of fragile or unworthy authority :
Custom :
The imperfection of undisciplined senses :
Concealment of ignorance by ostentation of seeming wisdom.

Furthermore, as to what truth is, I will say that, apart from the truths of our most holy faith which are of divine revelation and therefore not to be questioned, the truth is that which every man may acquire from the apprehensive nature of perfectly cultivated senses: or, as Zeno the Stoic saith, the test of truth is the Kataleptic Phantasm. For this cause, o Prospero, I will write history for thee from the evidence of my proper senses alone, and

---

[1] This would be Br. Roger Bacon, O.F.M.

not from the idle reports of ungoverned and ungovernable tongues.

I will choose to write the history of the day on which I was delivered from disability, of the day on which Alexander, magnificent, invincible, made me what I now am. I will write the history of my fortunate day. On that day, many things were done in which I had no little share. Of these things I will write. But, to know the history of that day absolutely as the Ruler of Olympos[1] knoweth it, needs must that The Prince[2] and the Cardinal of Ferrara, and Prince Gioffredo Borgia of Squillace, and innumerable other persons, should be moved as I am moved, and should be capable as I am capable, and should write as I will write. Nevertheless, seeing that none of these have written, thou

---

[1] *Regnator Olympi* is Don Tarquinio's designation of The Deity.

[2] I am led to believe that this is he whom Machiavelli called The Prince—viz., Cesare (Borgia), Cardinal of Valencia, and later Duke of Valentinois.

shalt be content to take the history of that day from me, thy loving father. It will be a good enough history, seeing that I assisted at its making and that I wish to tell the truth.

Thou shalt know, o virginal Prospero,[1] that, in the year MCCCCLXXXXV after the Admirable Parturition of the Mother-Maid, our house was suffering for its sins. For *xij* years before, on the ninth day of the kalends of March, mine uncle and our baron Madonno Francesco, the same who was the model for Messer Simone Fiorentini's[2] image of our primate Saint George of Seriphos, had been stabbed in a brawl by one of the infamous Dellavalle. We instantly had leagued with Orsini against this our hereditary enemy

---

[1] This Prospero was born xiii Sept. 1513—*i.e.*, under the Sign *Virgo* and the Planet *Mercury*. He seems to have been of a singularly pure mind, very studious, and an excellent man of affairs. He left a great name behind him as cardinal, plenipotentiary, and nuncio; and as the introducer of tobacco into Italy.

[2] This sculptor was commonly known as Donatello. The image of St. George is at Florence.

and Colonna ; and had comported ourselves in
such wise that, during *iij* months, the blood of
those monsters befouled every gutter in the
City. But, when we were in the very article
of ridding this land of those reptiles, even as
Saint George our said progenitor ridded his
Isle of Seriphos of the pterodactyl, for very few
of them remained alive, then our Lord the
Paparch[1] reinforced them with the bands of
His Own house of Dellarovere and with those
of Riarj to which He was allied by the marriage
of His sister. Then indeed we tolerated many
evils. His said Sanctity expelled us all from
the City, man, woman, priest, and child,
encumbering us with the Great Ban so that we
never should return ; and, further, He ordained the demolition of our palace on
Catinari.[2] It was done ; and for this same
cause my cousin now buildeth that new palace
where we shall live.

---

[1] Xystus the Fourth (Francesco Dellarovere).

[2] Piazza Catinari, where the earthenware dishes
came from.

Marcantonio, my said cousin, being mine equal in age, retired to Fiorenza. Being of a singular habit of mind, anxious to evade the society of most men, and not having a taste either for war or for letters, he became a disciple of Messer Lionardo da Vinci that miracle of genius, who loved him as Sokrates loved Phaidōn for his beautiful hair : with whom he studied the arts, fortifications, architecture, painting, and the construction of ingenious machines whereby men might fly with wings like bats or swim with webbed feet like tritons.

We of the junior branch made way to our castle of Deira by Squillace in the Kingdom,[1] which thou never hast seen but shalt see. That demesne formerly was denominated Greater Greece,[2] by cause that while yet the City was no more than a cluster of Alban shepherds' huts on Campidoglio[3] and Latium a

---

[1] "Lo Regno"—*i.e.*, Southern Italy, the Kingdom of Naples.　　　[2] ἡ μεγαλη Ἑλλας.

[3] The space between the two peaks of the Capitoline Hill.

kingdom, numbers cf our progenitors took
ship from Athens, violet-crowned, immortal,
and founded states and cities on these shores.

But at Deira we fortified ourselves, drawing
fighting men and youths apt to war from
among the natives ; and, by cause that the
arteries of these were filled with the blood of
Athenian heroes mixed with the blood of those
fierce Northmen, who also settled in our
vicinity about the time when our castle was
a-building, that is to say about the year ML
since our Fructiferous Redemption, our potency
became superior to that of all other barons of
the said Kingdom.   But, though we lived in
peace, shewing ourselves rather dangerous to
any who would have been our enemies, yet we
maintained ourselves with all the incessant
stringency of siege, at first in preparation for
an assault by the Riarj, with our ancient foes,
(which never was delivered, I suppose by cause
that the whole orb of earth knew that we were
very gravely to be feared being driven to bay ;)
and even afterward, when Xystus had migrated

to The Lord and the Riarj and the Dellarovere
had lost their predominance, we abated none of
our precautions, seeing that we were ignorant
concerning the manner in which the new
paparch Innocent[1] would use Himself toward
us.

In those *xij* years, o Prospero, thy father
passed from the care of nurses to boyhood and
even to the gate of adolescence. I am not to
intreat of those years now, nor of the manner
in which I spent them. But I will say that,
having something of the solitary habit of
Marcantonio, and being not entirely engrossed
by martial exercises or by human letters as all
my fellows were, I learned to think; and
thinking made me chafe, by cause that I
deemed it to be a terrible sacrilege against the
Maker of the World that I should be compelled to waste my life among the rustics of
Deira, I being fit in mind and body to equal
any patrician in the City. My syllogism
was the syllogism of the Alexandrian mages :

---

[1] Innocent the Eighth (Giambattista Cibo).

Intelligence must be Active :

God is Intelligent :

Therefore, of His Nature He must create :
for a force which engendereth nothing
is not a force.

God is the Creator :

In His Own Image He created Me :

Therefore, I also must Create.

But at Deira I was as a bird in a cage, as a
prisoner in a dungeon, as a scorpion in a circle
of fire :[1] nor was there any release for me.
Wherefore the new adolescence of me,
exquisite, ebullient, very grievously did chafe.

But by chance, on the festival of Saint
Valentine in the year MCCCCLXXXXV, there
occurred to me the Most Illustrious Lord
Cardinal-Δ. of Santa Lucia *in Silice* alias *in*

---

[1] Don Tarquinio seems to have been born under
the Sign *Scorpio* and the Planet *Mars :* which accounts
for his queer character. I think this expression to be
an allusion to the scorpion's well-known practice of
committing suicide by stinging itself when surrounded
by fire.

Orfea, the Prince Ippolito d'Este of Ferrara.
He came with an admirable company out of
Syracuse where he had been buying wrestlers:
for he was very curious in every kind of human
monster, and his collection of athletes was
without rival. He himself also was by way of
being abnormal: for he was of the age of *xvij*
years, and during *ij* years he had worn the
vermilion hat. He was tall of frame and
supple of sinew and mighty of limb, having
fortified his adolescence with archery and other
exercises. Grace and charm bloomed on the
face of him. His olive-coloured skin glowed
with healthful pallor. His bright black eyes
gleamed with grave tranquillity, meriting
praises. His whole aspect was most basilical.
He was an expert swimmer ; and, with whatso-
ever weapons he adroitly strove, he did inure
himself to heat and cold and night-long
vigils.[1]

Thou shalt know, o my rosy Prospero, that

---

[1] Ciacconius, in his *Lives of the Pontiffs*, seems to
have availed himself of this description of the Cardinal
of Ferrara.

there are two kinds of beauty, *videlicet* the
beauty of the body and the beauty of the soul.
The latter is to be preferred: for it is per-
manent ; and he who possesseth psychical
beauty is like the immortal gods, divine ones
inhabiting heavenly mansions. Yet this kind
of beauty is not easily perceived. Wherefore
the possession of the other kind is much to be
desired: by cause that physical beauty maketh
the world to turn round and to stand at gaze,
whereby perception of psychical beauty, if any
there be, is facilitated. Hence, physical beauty
is the more important: although, unless to it
be added psychical beauty, it is liable to become
invalid when its first effect should have faded.
But the Cardinal of Ferrara had both kinds of
beauty, even as I the present scribe have both
kinds of beauty.

When we first looked upon each other, our
attention was arrested by means of the sense of
sight: but, when words had passed, we recog-
nized each other as being of equal texture,
even as one star doth recognize another cross-

ing the firmament of heaven, or as travellers returning to their dear homes recognize their kindred standing on the threshold greeting.

After many words had been spoken: for, as soon as the glances of our eyes first clashed together, striking the spark of sympathy, whereby a certain fire burned in our minds, and as Harmodios and Aristogeitōn loved each other so did we : then the mighty Ippolito thus addressed me :

"It is not meet that such an one should be chained to this rock of Deira, where the vultures of impotent desire and of annulled energy consume thine heart and liver."

Thus he spoke: but there was a plan in his mind, perceiving which I responded, saying :

"Only the successor of Him, Who chained Us and Our house with the Great Ban, is able to deliver; and that is the Paparch Alexander."[1]

---

[1] Alexander the Sixth (Rodrigo de Borja y Borja, commonly called Borgia).

Ippolito answered me again, saying :

"We Ourself are in the grace of the said Alexander, magnificent, invincible. Moreover the Great Ban will not run in thy despite so long as that thou shalt be in Our company : for, where Este is, Ferrara is ; and Rome hath no jurisdiction in Ferrara."

His saying was a true one. Wherefore, having collected my familiars, with a joyful heart I turned my back upon Deira ; and anon, with the Cardinal of Ferrara, I rode to Rome. As we rode, we conversed concerning many things, in order that the beauty of our souls might be manifested : nor did we omit to exhibit the beauty of our bodies in feats of strength and agility. It appeared that, though I had not such irresistible strength as Ippolito had, nevertheless my limberness and quickness of eye gave me no cause to blush while we contended. But, when our alliance was confirmed by the discovery of our admirable qualities, we gave names to each other, as the manner was. To Ippolito, I gave the name

Hebe,[1] on account of his *xvij* years. To me, he gave the name Sideynes,[2] on account of my *xv* years. And so conversing and contending, we reached the City.

It was agreed that I should live as a guest in the Estense Palace, until such time when Ippolito should find occasion for speaking of me to our Lord the Paparch. And so it was. But, as soon as we had invaded the City, I became conscious that I had exchanged one prison for another: for, on account of the Great Ban, it was not convenient that I should go out from the Estense Palace, unless a decurion[3] of the cardinalitial familiars attended and surrounded me.

Thus, I was precluded from seeking such adventures as my youth and my spirit required. Now and then, I accepted the restraint: in order that I might see the world's metropolis,

---

[1] $\dot{\eta}\beta\eta$ = youthful prime (in Sparta, the eighteenth year).

[2] $\sigma\iota\delta\epsilon\upsilon\nu\eta\varsigma$ = a youth of fifteen to sixteen years (Laconian).

[3] Ten soldiers and a lieutenant.

of which I myself was no mean citizen. But
the estate of my procession terribly irked me ;
and I would not have gone out any more,
save for a maid whom I espied on the third
day ; and she was thy proper mother, o Prospero. For, when I saw the tender girlishness
of her, and her blue-black hair, and her blue-
black eyes, and her rosy flesh, which was so
bright and pure that I knew it to be soft
and firm and cool to touch, then the fire of
love was kindled in my dear breast; and I
yearned after her. But her very name was
hidden from me: nor might I ask it of any,
for I was environed by my guards, and she
was in the train of a princess. Her gait
proclaimed her nobility. She appeared to be
of equal age with me. For which causes, I
pervaded the City at all hours in hope of an
auspicious encounter.

Once I scattered primroses low at the feet
of her beauty. She gazed modestly downward : but I looked where I loved.

II

THAT was the third day.

The eighth was my fortunate day. I will set down the history of the said day, a.d. *vij* Kal. Mar., being the day of Mars in the year MCCCCLXXXXV.

Divine Phoibos was finishing his course, and his radiant horses were about to plunge into the ocean-stream, when the Most Illustrious Lord Cardinal-Δ. of Santa Lucia *in Silice* alias *in Orfea*, Prince Ippolito d'Este of Ferrara, with me, Prince Tarquinio Georgio Drakontoletes Poplicola di Hagiostayros,[1] came

---

[1] The gentleman's actual surname, of course, was Santacroce : but, being rabidly infected with the mania of his epoch for Greek, he must needs give it the Greek form of Ἁγιοσταυρος. Regarding his frequent allusions to Saint George of Seriphos as his progenitor, the curious may remember that it was

from a certain meadow beyond the Milvian Bridge[1] where we had been playing at great-ball.[2] A pair of patrician pages had played on his side, which was red ; and another pair played on my side, which was blue : but the red were victorious. I cannot remember the names of the said pages : nor is it of importance that I should remember them. Many persons have thrown the great-ball since Deykalion threw stones ; and the names of the throwers have gone down into oblivion. These throwers were among those.

Having come to the bank of Tiber, we

Perseys of Seriphos who slew a dragon (pterodactyl ?), that Perseys' mother Danae founded Ardea in Latium, that Publius Valerius Poplicola came to Rome from Ardea, that the house of Santacroce descends from him, and that the armorials of Santacroce are the armorials of Saint George, argent a cross potent gules. From which considerations a somewhat startling theory may be formed.

[1] Now called Ponte Molle.

[2] Pallone, a deliriously scientifically ferocious game common in Italy.

ascended the cardinalitial barge. Indian oarsmen propelled it ; and the colour of their
flesh resembled the colour of a field of ripe
wheat when as some delicate zephyr sways the
stems in the sunlight not more than half re-
vealing poppies : but their eyes were like
pools of ink, fathomless, upon glittering
mother o' pearl, very beautiful, and quite un-
intellectual. Servitors crowded amidships.
Turkish arbalisters and halberdiers from
Ferrara manned the bulwarks. Pages, in
liveries resembling vermilion skins from toe to
throat and wrist, bearing armorials on their
tabards, displayed at the prow the double-
cross, golden, and the high Estense gonfalon,
in order to teach discretion. For, cardinals
like Ippolito, and princes like Tarquinio,
risked life whenever they would play at
great ball, in those old days when the Keltic
barbarians of Gaul were occupying half the
City on the one side of Tiber, while the
Paparch Alexander was being beleaguered
in the Castle of Santangelo on the other.

For this cause Ippolito displayed his state, so that any man of evil mind, presumptuous, who should be tempted of the devil to molest us, might know that he would incur the ban of Holy Mother Church for molesting a cardinal not less than the ban of Ferrara for molesting an Este.

The air above the river was growing chilly. We who were heated with the game needed to continue in action, that we might evade perils of ague or of fever or of the Pest, most pernicious. Wherefore I wrestled as vigorously as possible with Ippolito inside the vermilion curtains of the canopied poop. But his great strength reduced my suppleness to no price ; and he threw me once and twice and six times, till he was weary of easy victories : but I was weary of the carpet.

Abaft Ripetta,[1] came one in a little boat with rumours : with whom we instantly collogued. It was said that some sort of a peace had been

---

[1] The port where the agricultural produce from Umbria was landed.

patched-up. It was said that the Keltic King was about to relinquish the City.

Ippolito's mind became inflamed with desire of inquiry. Wherefore, having crossed the river, we descended from the barge ; and made haste toward Vatican, in order that we might get the news from that side.

As we hurried through the streets, mine heart was sad and disconsolate in my breast, by cause of my secret longing and by cause of mine ill-used body ; and I was oblivious of all other things.

Ippolito perceived my grief, and set himself to console me, as we walked along : but he knew not all the causes of my distress. He spoke only of the Great Ban, which indeed weighed heavily, and moreover it was the root and source of all mine ill. For, had it not been for that grave impediment, I should have been a free prince ; and, with my freedom, I could have won the desire of my soul, and also could have used my body to advantage. Thus he spoke: but I passed, from grieving over mine unknown maid and my bruised flesh, into most profound trouble by cause of my disability. And that trouble was so sore that very soon it changed into furious despair. I would do : but I could not do, by cause that I might not do. To myself I seemed useless. I was merely a bandit. Yet I got no joy of my banditry as other bandits did, by cause that I was too foolish or too wise to comport myself as a bandit.

Blood was blinding mine eyes at these thoughts; and my lips quivered fiercely. Thus to Vatican I came, in a passion of rage.

III

I SAW those great stone stairs leading to the long fortified gallery which extends from the Apostolic Palace to the Castle of Santangelo. I saw the porphyry-coloured lines of paparchal men-at-arms which guarded them. I also saw the porphyry-coloured knots of chamberlains and pages and prelates which clustered upon them. All around me were voices and the noise of movement. Cardinals and bishops and barons, each with his company, continually were arriving and ascending the stairs and disappearing along the gallery above, or emerging therefrom and descending and departing.

All this time, Ippolito was pouring sympathetic words into my deaf ears. As he left me, I contrived to hear him say:

"Be of good heart, O Sideynes, for thy chance may be near even now. Fortune never ceaseth to turn her wheel ; and what is down to-day may be up to-morrow."

Then he climbed the stair, attended by his pages ; and I was left alone.

I stood by a window in the hall, very sad. Our *ij* decurions remained, waiting in my vicinity, but not so near as to intrude upon my secret. Mine heart began to weep within my breast, silently, very bitterly : but the crowds which came in and the crowds which went out were ignorant of my grief. To the genuinely aggrieved, there is nothing more distracting (and consoling) than the knowledge that he is keeping his grievance to himself.

Anon, a certain princess entered, attended by a galaxy of maids-of-honour, all chattering like jays, very flippant. She was most virginal and young, with a long sheet of shining yellow hair flowing loosely from a garland of jacinths. Her robe of mulberry-coloured silk was embroidered with gold herring-bones. The paparchal pages swept us against the wall to make a passage for her. I took one by the ear, demanding the lady's name for a very valid reason. Having said that she was Madonna Lucrezia Borgia-Sforza, the daughter of the Paparch's Sanctity, the wife of the Tyrant of Pesaro, a pearl of women, lovely and good, gentle and courteous to all, anon he threatened me with penalties for my abuse of his ear. But I consoled him with *iij* silver ouches shaped like herons which I tore out of my cloak; and, having pushed through the throng, I made a very low obeisance to the princess : for I wished to be seen of her in whose train I myself had noted my maid.

When Madonna Lucrezia had given me a frank and simple look of admiration, for I was not unnotable in a knitted habit like a skin of nacre-coloured silk embroidered with a flight of silver herons,[1] she also climbed the stairs and disappeared : but her maids-of-honour waited in the gallery.

I was standing below, strenuously looking upward. Courtiers came forward up there,

---

[1] The word Ardea signifies "a heron." The city of Ardea is the cradle of the race of Santacroce.

pairing with the girls, strutting to and fro like a troop of apes and a muster of peacocks. One of the maids had no companion. She was walking by herself.

An enormous baron, one of the loyal Cesarini, came from the gallery. His company gathered round him as he began the descent of the stair. The solitary maid also stepped down in his train, just when I was sinking again into my melancholy; and then I saw no more of anyone, but only her.

Her sea-blue robe was girdled by great cat's-eyes set in gold. Her mane of blue-black hair floated around her from a coronal of sea-blue beryls. There was a modest look of seeking in her eyes, half-veiled by lovely lashes. Tender blushes brightened her diaphanous flesh. I watched her very cautelously, maintaining my dejected attitude by the window, using all the powers of my will to draw her to me. Several times she passed me as she paced the hall. Anon she stayed by me, lifting her lashes, fulfilling me with the light of her regard; and she said :

" O Madonnino, why art thou so unutterably sad ?"

I wrenched myself from my distress : and comported myself as one to whom a divine vision is vouchsafed, letting a look of recognition gradually come into mine eyes. So I went to her ; and drew her into the embrasure of the window, where the mailed backs of my decurion walled us off from the passers-by. And, on my two firm knees, I told her that I had loved her since first I saw her in the City.

She was not angry : but sweetly tender, modest, not unwilling. Her mood brightened mine ; and mine heart became as blithe as the sea at dawn in spring. She was not mine ; but she was to be had for the asking : for which cause I continued to speak. I said that I hitherto had had no means of approaching her : that I even now was ignorant of her name ; and I used the sacred language of lovers.

She begged me to rise, lest some passer-by should misunderstand me ; and her eyes darted up the stairs to the other maids with their partners. She was very young, and perhaps a little terrified by the violence of love, though she by no means was for flying from it. I stood up; and, by cause that I most fervently regarded her, she let her eyelids droop a little while she responded to me, telling me her name and condition. Anon she used a new stratagem in the sweet affray, demanding that I should speak about myself. So, I was driven back into the citadel of my sadness, mine assault being prevented. She pushed me closer, persisting, gently urging me.

Anon I told her how that our house had been *xij* years in exile, notwithstanding that we were the most noble patricians in the Golden Book of Rome; and I spoke of Saint George the Dragon-slayer of Seriphos, of the Great Ban, of our razed palace, of our baron fooling at Fiorenza. I said that I was a scion of the younger branch, and innocent of the murders which had caused us to be banned; and I told her of my breeding, with all other matters necessary to be known by her. I gave her notice of mine arts and parts. There I was to serve her, as she could see, young, strong, well-instructed, not uncomely, and burning for an opportunity of doing deeds. I also spoke of Ippolito, my friend, who had brought me to the City in search of that opportunity which was not at Deira.

She, with divine tenderness, feared for my safety. I gave her confidence again, reciting the precautions observed and the privileges enjoyed among the Estense familiars. But, by side of these things, I bade her to know that I as yet was not a notable person upon whom our Lord the Paparch well might execute justice. Further, I said that Alexander so far had not manifested special virulence toward mine house. We were bandits when He began to reign. So He found us. The Great Ban had been laid on us by His predecessors; and, if He so willed, He could annul it. Wherefore I had taken the risk, for the sake of meeting an opportunity. And I showed her how that Ippolito, being in the Paparch's favour, was watching daily for a fortunate moment in which to plead my case. Not

that I wished to sue for favours : but I was
seeking an opportunity for doing some signal
service, which should merit and compel paparchal approbation. I preferred to help myself.
But, until my disability should have been removed, I was (so I said) like a prisoner in
chains, unable to use myself.

She moved a little nearer to me, lifting the
sweet deep wells of her eyes for me to bathe
in ; and she said :

" O Madonnino, how I pity, how I pity !"

But I instantly responded, bending my
proper eyes to hers, saying :

" O Madonnina, pity is akin to love."

And, at the word, I saw mine image in-
shrined within those mirrors of her soul. It
was an omen, very fortunate, very invigorating.
If Hersilia loved me, that nerved me ; and I
would persevere. So I said.

She wished to speak for me to Madonna
Lucrezia : saying that that one was beneficent
to everybody and all-powerful with her Most
Holy Father. But I denied her. A man

ought to raise himself and not to owe his fortunes to women. That was my sentence. I also said that Hersilia was like the angel who formerly delivered the Paparch Saint Peter from chains. She had made me strong to free myself. Nothing more was necessary except a little patience and a fortunate event.

She gave her hand to mine hot kisses. It was as dainty as a baby's.

At that moment, Ippolito and Madonna Lucrezia appeared together in the gallery; and began the descent of the stairs. There was a sudden collecting of companies. Long-legged pages darted hither and thither with much confusion; and anon I was by Ippolito's side striding down Borgo.

He had no news for me. Our Lord the Paparch was playing with chess against His favourite page out of Spain;[1] and only had whispered *ij* words to the cardinal. What those *ij* words

---

[1] This perhaps would be the Pierotto Calderon whom Cesare is said to have murdered so very romantically indeed.

were, was Ippolito's secret. Nor had I any news for him. What I had heard from my maid, was my secret. Together we went in silence, pondering our proper affairs.

So we ascended the waiting barge ; and proceeded down Tiber, rapt in meditation. And the sun set in gold.

IIII

WHEN the barge had swung free of the shoal of smaller boats by the quay, and had attained mid-stream, Ippolito anon emerged from his thoughts. I also emerged from mine. There was a gleam of hilarity in his black-eyed glance. I returned it. It was understood that we were setting trouble aside for the moment, and engaging each other in some feat of daring, as our manner was.

Having cast off his vermilion robes, Ippolito blessed his body ; and forthwith smoothly plunged into the river, strongly swimming with a huge leap sideways and a circular sweep of alternate arms and a double downward thrust of his mighty haunches. I for a few moments watched him, while I strengthened my proper arms by swinging the heavy arm-shields, wooden, cylindrical, studded with

D

square knops, which we had used in our game of great-ball. Anon, having made ready, I climbed on the high shoulders of the steersman, standing there till Ippolito saw my whiteness; and so I dived into the barge's wake, and swam.

The oarsmen diminished their speed to ours; and we swam between the right bank, where our Lord the Paparch kept His court in the Castle of Santangelo, and the left bank, where the army of the Keltic king inravished half the City. We continued swimming together under the new Xystine Bridge, and under the Cestian Bridge, and by the Island,[1] until the barge was moored by the Estense quay in Trastevere.

Gigantic jatraleiptai,[2] which Ippolito got out of Morocco, attended us when we climbed inboard. Their chestnut-coloured bodies were girdled with azure-green. Using pure oil of olives in which violets were macerated, they

---

[1] The Island of Saint Bartholomew in the Tiber.
[2] This is Don Tarquinio's word for shampooers.

imparted friction with their hands to our chilled flesh. When my skin had the rosy glow of pomegranates, they robed me in a cloak of vair of nut-brown squirrels: but Ippolito muffled himself in the ermine and vermilion of his great-cloak, covering his head with a coif of the same. Chamberlains with *vj* torches went before him, *iij* went before me, when we left the barge and entered the palace. Our teeth chattered with cold, preventing articulate speech: but our bodies were warm.

There was an immense crowd of familiars along the quay and by the water-gate, free-lances from Ferrara, Gothic halberdiers, Dacian slingers, red-haired Skythian wrestlers very gigantic, roe-footed runners from Utter Britain, North African Moors, Ethiopic athletes, Indian acrobats, all selected for some singular physical beauty or capability. The crowd, as I have said, seemed to be immense: but considering that Ippolito was a prince as well as a cardinal, a family of merely *cccc* persons was by no means over-abundant.

Many barons and many sacredly purpled persons are well known to keep much larger families : but Ippolito cared more for quality than for quantity, and he cared nothing at all for ostentation or display. This trait of his character was very pleasing to me: for I myself at all times would rather have those exquisite things which no other prince hath, than a superfluity of those things which are common to all.

The water-gate, iron-barred, iron-shielded, clanged behind us. Armed footmen lined the stair. Slight vermilion pages, patrician on this side, plebeian on that, made obeisance in the *xv* antechambers. A bevy of delicate youngsters, whose hair glittered like cocoons in candlelight, joined our progress. Ippolito was wont to pay *cccmd* golden sequins[1] for one of these specimens of The Creator's handiwork ; and he had collected no more than *viiij*. He told me this, seeing how greatly I admired them ; and he described

---

[1] About £7,000, or $30,000.

the difficulty which his agents had had in finding them, for there was no blemish on them from sole to crown. Thus conversing, we passed the wardrobe, where the master waited with his grooms and our gentlemen; and so we parted to go to our bathing-chambers. From this description, o Prospero, thou shalt know how a cardinal kept state in the days of thy father's youth. But I will continue, that no single thing which I did on that day may be hidden from thee.

Well-grown pages, girt with white napkins, spread the floor-sheets and sponged my flesh with warm water, rubbing me with lupin-meal, alkaline, emollient. Having poured cold jasmine-water over me, and dried me with fine flax, they indued me with knitted under-garb of soft wool, swathing my wet hair with cloths. Wrapped in a woollen night-gown, I encountered Ippolito similarly arrayed in the wardrobe. The grooms produced various habits; and our pages deftly did them on us. Ippolito's grand legs were sheathed in silk

hosen, tyrianthine-coloured. A loose doublet
of the same covered his body. It was open
on the breast and the long wide sleeves, shewing the laces and embroidery of his smock.
His poignard dangled from a golden belt
formed of linked dryades and naiades. His
cap and his shoes were vermilion. His
pectoral cross was hidden in his smock ; and
his chain was set with those periapts which
procure fearlessness and avert drowning, passion,
incubi and succubi, *videlicet* carnelian, jasper,
topaz, coral. And I must not omit to record
that the sapphire of his ring, worth *dc* sequins,[1]
was engraved with a figure of the Heroic
Herakles strangling the Nemean Lion, which
inchanteth against colic and gaineth favour.
But I, on my part, chose to wear no smock
that night, preferring a certain habit of white
silk which clung to my contours. It was
shaped like an inverted chevron on breast
and back, with broidered bands of pearls on
silver ; and I chose it by cause that I could

---

[1] About £1,200, or $6,000.

breathe more freely when my throat was bare, for mine heart was very full of the joy which cometh to him who hath done well with his body. Indeed I hardly could stand still while the pages very carefully rubbed the delicate fabric on me, smoothing the wrinkles : but, when this was done, I knew that I had chosen rightly, for this habit was no restraint to me. A pointed belt of linked silver medals engraved with the loves of Leykippe and Kleitophonta bound a brief close flounce of silver-banded silk round my loins; and my boots were of white buckskin, clasped with silver at an handsbreadth below my knees. They also brought me a white silk cap proud with plumes, and a thick cloak of white velvet reversed with ermine.

So I stood, while Ippolito praised me, saying that I resembled Messer Verrocchio's lithe thalerose image of David carven of shimmering mother o' pearl. Concerning which same image, and concerning also the other image of David by Messer Donatello, I took occasion to narrate the tragicomedy of the said images, and of the *ij* adolescents of Deira named Baldonero Fioravanti and Rufo Drudodimare, and of their doings with the white-faced cardinal.[1] And the same history I shall put in an appendix,[2] seeing that no more than the mention of it is pertinent to this present history. But my discourse was so pleasing to Ippolito that, when I had made an end of speaking, he sent to me a page with a tray of rings for mine acceptance. Wherefrom I chose *vj* for the adornment of my thumbs and my first-fingers and my third-fingers : *videlicet* a cockatrice, intagliate in green jasper, for averting the evil eye : a fair boy's head well-combed, intagliate in smaragd, for preserving joy : an Apollino with a necklace of herbs, intagliate in heliotrope, which conferreth invisibility when anointed with marigold-juice : the Kythereia and Ares, intagliate in chal-

---

[1] Rafaele Sansoni-Riarj, struck pallid at sixteen when he was expecting to be murdered by the Medici.

[2] Which his present tralator takes leave to omit.

cedonyx, for gaining victories: the Anadyo-
mene, intagliate in sea-blue beryl, fine, brilliant,
very large, also for gaining victories: a silver
ring set through on all sides with toadstone
and ass-hoof, for augmenting manlihood and
for protection against venom ; and, having
thanked Ippolito, I sent him the rest in the tray.

The patrician pages, who stood in our
shadows, quietly quarrelled among themselves
while they filled our burses with perfumes,
comfit-boxes, kerchieves, combs, mirrors, amu-
lets, tablets, rosaries, and other gear. We
struck them in the rear with spatulas from time
to time. Nor would we permit them to affix
the said burses to our belts : for our forms
would have been falsified thereby. Wherefore,
they perforce were compelled to carry them,
attending us closely, buffeted as occasion
served. But we sat resting in arm-chairs,
while the grooms covered us with sheets with
fringes, drying and combing and scenting our
raven-hued and yellow-silver hair.

For our solace, a chamberlain admitted a

pair of chaplains in black cymars with an arch-
luth and a book of hours. They kneeled, and
intoned vespers with completorium. At the
Sign and Et fidelium animae, the bells of the
City began to sound in a new manner, strange
then to me, but familiar enough to thee,
o Prospero, *videlicet iij* strokes, *iiij* strokes,
v strokes, *i* stroke, *xiii* strokes in all.

I looked with inquiry toward Ippolito. He
smiled : for he had been at the heart of things
that day ; and he said that it was the new
ordinance of our Lord the Paparch.

Our coverings instantly were removed. Two
vermilion cushions were placed before us. All
sank on the knees. The Cardinal of Ferrara
intoned, in honour of the Fructiferous Incarna-
tion ; and we responded to him, saying

V. Angelus Domini nŭtiavit Mariae :
R. Et cŏcepit de Spiritu Sācto.
            Aue Maria, etc.

V. Ecce ăcilla Domini :
R. Fiat michi secŭdu' Verbu' Tuu'
            Aue Maria, etc.

V. Et Verbu' Caro factu' est :

R. Et habitauit i' nobis.

          Aue Maria, etc.

V. Ora pro nobis, Sācta Dei Genitrix :

R. Ut digni efficiamur promissionibus Christi.

V. Oremus.   Gratia' Tua', quaesumus, Domine, mêtibus nostris ĭfúde, ut Qui, āgelo nŭtiăte, Christ Filj Tui Ĭcarnatione' cognovimus, per Passione' Ejus et Cruce' ad Resurrectionis Gloria' perducamur. Per Eŭde' Christu' Dominu' nostru' :

R. Amen.

V. ✠ Et fideliu' animae per Misericordia' Dei requiescāt i' pace :

R. Amen.

It was the first hour of night.[1]

Now, the day which for me for ever is marked with a white stone, fortune-bringing, the great day of my life was begun.

---

[1] About 6 p.m.   Each day was counted to begin at sunset of the previous night.

V

I will tell thee, o Prospero, of the Estense
Palace : for it is impossible for thee to see it
with thy proper sea-blue eyes, by cause that
it was pulled down in the year before thy
birth, after the miraculous picture appeared on
the garden-wall ; and hath given place to the
new church of Theotokos with the new
streets.[1]

It was a gigantic oblong, extending from the

---

[1] This would seem to indicate the locality of this
mysterious palace : for a miraculous Madonna was
found on a garden-wall in Trastevere A.D. 1497, and
the church of Santa Maria dell' Orto (Saint Mary of
the Garden) was built over it A.D. 1512, the year
before the birth of Cardinal Prospero Santacroce.
The palace, therefore, must have stood upon a slice of
the site now occupied by St. Michael's Hospice and
the barracks of the Bersaglieri, with a water-gate on
Ripa Grande.

river-bank to the said garden-wall, having the
grove of the Divine Furina on the one side, and
Saint Cecilia and Saint Mary of the Chapel on
the other. It was neither so fine nor so large
as that new palace which my cousin and our
baron Marcantonio is about to build on Catinari : but it was fine and large enough for
a foreign cardinal. One end of the oblong
abutted on Tiber, where was the great barbacan
and the water-gate ; and it was divided into
iiij equal-sided courts by the hall and the
audience-chamber and the chapel. The ex-
terior walls were fortifications *v* braccie[1] in
thickness, where little window-slits lighted only
galleries and stairs. Who builded it, I do not
know : but, when it was pulled down we recog-
nized it as the work of a master-builder, cyclo-
pean, absolute. All the chief apartments were
on the first floor. Below were kitchens,
cellars, prisons, store-houses, military quarters.
Above were *iij* floors for the familiars and the

---

[1] 12 feet 11 inches. The braccia was 2 feet
7 inches long.

athletes. The first court from the gate was
allotted to the soldiers and servitors : the
second, to the gentlemen and pages : the third
to the men of letters and to the illustrious,
nobilities, supernities, celsitudes, tranquillities,
magnificences, sublimities : the fourth was the
court of the women, where the wives and
daughters of the familiars cooked the food and
made or mended clothes, pent from boys
and adolescents savage or military, in suitable
seclusion beyond the ruota.[1] A flat roof, with
machicolated battlement, crowned the pile,
chiefly fortified, but also providing a terrace,
d braccie[2] in total length, *l* braccie[3] in width,
for Ippolito's recreations.

These things being understood, I will continue the history.

When we stood up ready to proceed from
the wardrobe, all the people came and made

---

[1] A huge revolving cupboard, by which means
communication was made.

[2] 473 yards 1 foot 10 inches.

[3] 43 yards 2 inches.

their genuflections. The pages with the cardinalitial double-cross and the Estense gonfalon went before. The gentlemen followed after, playing with their budding upper-lips. These were quite useless persons, not even showy, and only included in the family in order that they might learn manners. I never have had gentlemen in my proper family : for I prefer pages and servitors to whom I can speak and who will respond to me in turn. I would rather be surrounded by barbarians, as Ippolito generally was, than by these silent simpering youths who are merely noble. And as for myself, rather than be a gentleman in another baron's family, I would prefer to be a farmer. And, as I will for myself, so also I will for my dear son. Note it, o Prospero.

The chamberlains preceded us with the *vj* torches and the *iij*. As we passed down the *iiij* stairs which led into the first gallery, a chamberlain slipped on a patch of tallow, which had dropped from a rush-light badly placed in the sconce on the wall. He was a very fat

man ; and his hosen split on the ham-bone :
at whose discomfiture we laughed, but Ippolito
was promising a thrashing for someone.

In the private dining-room, I was moved
to give an inkling of mine hopes to Ippolito,
continuing to whisper until we had passed
through the state withdrawing-room into the
hall. He sighed when I spoke of my maid ;
and suddenly smiled, as one who locketh the
box of his trouble when his friend unlocketh
his box of joy. It appeared to me that Ippolito was not ignorant of an experience similar
to mine : but the importance of my proper
affairs prevented me from placing inquiries
concerning his.

My discourse was interrupted by the pages
at the door of the hall presenting the em-
bossed gold basin with the ewer of tepid rose-
water and diapered towels, while we washed
our fingers reciting the Psalm *I will wash mine
hands in innocency*. Our seats on the dais were
canopied by the vermilion baldaquin, Ippolito's being on a step above mine. Below on

our right, was the table of the chaplains and the men of letters who knew the *iiij* human languages, *videlicet* Greek, Roman, Tuscan, Hebrew. Below on our left, was the table of the general comptroller of estates, the secretaries, the chief steward, the auditor, the notary, the datary, the captain and lieutenants of the guard, the herald, the physician, and the barber-chirurgeon. Lower down the hall were tables, large and long. At the middle table, where the salt-cellar divided patrician from plebeian, the gentlemen sat and the bevy of pages. The rest of the family was at the end of the hall. The plebeians each brought their daily portions from the canteen, *videlicet* *xvj* ounces of beef, *xx* ounces of fine or coarse bread according to condition, a pint and a half of wine, pieces of their monthly pounds of cheese. All through the meal, they looked lickerishly toward the dais, thinking of their chances of our gentle leavings.

Wax torches, *v* in number, escorted each dish from the ruota to the carving-table; *v*

E

others illumined the tables of the patricians :
cool, dim, twinkling wicks floating on oil in
brazen lamps, and the blaze of the logs on
the hearth, gave light to the rest. The reflections of these in the panels of the walls and
roof, oaken, wax-shining, resembled golden stars
in a brown sea.

·As I and Ippolito spread the napkins on our
breasts for tying, there was some commotion
at the pages' table. It was seen that, not
content with their own napkin, they had stolen
also the one pertaining to the gentlemen, which
napkin one of the last retrieved with a little
violence. We only saw the short struggle,
and we only heard the indignant advice to the
robbers that they should use their caps and
sleeves like the plebeians.

Ippolito demanded of me whether, in my
judgment, such advice was suitable for young
boys. I responded saying that it was indecorous, and that the adviser ought to be
dismissed. I forget whether this last was
done.

While the wan nervous venom-taster in black, who stood at Ippolito's left hand, was performing his office on the viands and on the wine, my flesh glowed with the stinging cold of my swim in Tiber and the subsequent ministrations of my pages. Ippolito was in a muse. But I looked at my face in my mirror; and saw happiness trying to shine there. I smoothed mine hair. I stretched my legs and arms. I felt strong. My bowels yearned to do some violent deed. But what deed? Ah, I did not know what deed to do. And I instantly slid from the height of bliss to the depth of misery. Oh, I indeed was properly unhappy.

As soon as the chaplains had finished intoning the prayers, I drank beef-and-barley broth from a silver bowl. It did not comfort me. I ate the beef from which the broth had been made. It was fibrous and dry. The brigands of the Campagna who, in those old days, used to steal half all imports sent to the City, must have been employed elsewhere that day : for roast pig and venison appeared on the carving table. I ate of both, being ravenously hungry and unwilling to waste time in talking to Ippolito about a stranger who was sitting at the table of the men of letters. But I said that a man who had an olive-coloured skin ought not to wear a pink and green gown ; and I have forgotten all else about the said stranger. The venison suited my taste, being fat and full of blood ; and I signed for a third platterful. Nor did I neglect the fried things, *videlicet* minced chicken livers in paste balls, goose-breasts in batter, cockscombs on lettuce, leeks parboiled and fried in oil, a dish of quails farced with figs. The goose-breasts and the cockscombs were the best. Every time when I paused to wash mine hands, I seemed to be sinking deeper in the mire of my melancholy.

I was plunging, sighing, into a gigantic salad : for I remembered that green-meat is as efficacious for whitening the skin as are blood-meats for rendering supple the sinews. But we heard the sudden ringing of horse-hooves in the court, and the champing of bitts, and the noise of an arrival. Then indeed the human tide at the end of the hall swept sideways, as Tiber surges when cloven by a galley's prow. A pursuivant and two vermilion chamberlains, each with a handful of lighted torches snatched from anywhere, precipitated themselves at the dais, announcing:

"The Exalted Potency of Prince Gioffredo Borgia of Squillace."

This prince, o Prospero, was then of mine own age: but he already had commanded *dccxl* free-lances in the war, and he already was *xj* months a benedick: while I, who could do nothing but fight and swim and run and speak Greek and write it and look much more like the David of Messer Verrocchio than Baldonero Fioravanti or than Rufo Drudodimare, I, I say, had no opportunity of doing anything. And I was most miserable. But I smiled, welcoming the guest: for he seemed to be a merry lad; and I admired the hardy contours of his form, precocious, voluptuous. Sulphur-coloured silk defined each line of him. The silver bands at his throat and wrists and hips were set with great cabochon emeralds no greener than his eyes which flashed between long lashes. His curly hair was as black as night. His flesh had the rosy clearness of carnation. His laughing mouth was as red as beef. He used himself with lively dignity as became the veritable son of our Lord the Paparch; and he came to greet us with a certain gesture. He said :

"Salute the father of a lovely girl, born a month ago at Naples, whom Our Most Holy Father yesterday hath baptized by the name Antonia."

The cellarers served a rich red wine of Nemi, full-bodied, well-sunned. Ippolito commanded them to bring moss-agate cups: in order that the Paparch's son might have security against venom.[1] While we drank,

---

[1] Moss-agate breaks when touched by poison.

those *ij* began to chatter of matters unknown to me.

I threw a cupful of wine in the face of the page with my basin, that I might make him as unhappy as I. He looked so meekly furious that I laughed as I washed my fingers before tasting the sweetmeats. But anon, remembering that the said page was noble and that I had hurt his honour, I sent him to fetch my two best swords. And, having slipped into the state withdrawing-room, I made him proud and happy by disarming him twice, scratching the back of his right hand. He was a bold boy, fearful of the blood of the grape, not of his own. But I returned to the cheese, more unhappy than before.

Chaplains intoned the long action of graces, ✠ Memoria' fecit mirabiliu' suoru' etc. I lingered over a conserve of quinces, which, said Ippolito, disperseth fumes and preventeth vapours from striking upwards ; and I chatted in Greek with Messer Pierettore Arrivabene below the dais, while Ippolito and the Borgia prince eagerly whispered.　When the familiars were gone out by the lower door, we *iij* washed our hands ; and went to take our ease in the secret chamber.　Singing boys followed our progress, mingling voices with archluths, quiet, clear, and low, music delightful to hear.

VI

THAT secret chamber, o Prospero, was circular
and very large. The walls and the vaulted roof
were covered with a veneer of ivory *iij* barleycorns in thickness, smoothly gleaming. Ivory
images of fauns and nymphs as large as life,
xj of the one, *x* of the other, stood on
ivory pedestals round the walls supporting the
cornice. The said cornice also was of ivory
carved with a dance of satyrs in basso rilievo.
Wax torches burned on tall gold candlesticks
placed on the floor between the images, except
in the spaces occupied by the ivory door and
the window. The last was furnished with a
balcony over Tiber; and shewed a view of
the City in darkening twilight. The floor
was covered by a very thick black carpet
from Byzantion.

Having washed our fingers at the gold

lavabo by the door, we composed ourselves on massive black velvet cushions, which were heaped up here and there upon the floor. Ippolito drew up a low ivory table ; and offered sweetmeats to us from a gold box, cursing meanwhile by cause that the pile of napkins for the night was lacking. In the midst of his objurgations, a servitor hurried in with an armful, depositing the same by the lavabo. Ippolito resumed his normal grave smile.

The men of letters swaggered in, bent on improving our minds. The first read the histories of Solon and Publius Valerius Poplicola with Parallel, from the βιοι παραλληλοι of Messer Ploytarchos : the second read a page of Messer Cicero's Oration for Caecina : the third declaimed the eighteenth canto of Messer Alighieri's Paradiso : the fourth intoned a lection from the Evangel of Saint John the Divine (whose Greek, o Prospero, is purer than that of the other Apostles, especially Saint Paul), and he used the second volume of that fine Bible which cost Duke Borso d'Este *mccclxxv* sequins.[1]

Prince Gioffredo became uneasy in his body : for he had not expected this kind of entertainment. Wherefore Ippolito conversed with him apart, while I became obedient to the mages who were my masters for the nonce : it being at all times my will, as it should be thine, o my mercurial son, to give as much care to the acquisition of mental superiority as to the acquisition of physical. I translated aloud into Tuscan a folio of the Phaidōn of Plato, that absolute work, and a breve of Messer Plinius from the new edition which Messer Pomponius Laetus had given to Ippolito.[2] Anon I meekly tolerated an adverse judgment of my weekly thesis, the absurd subject of which was The Irreducible Surd : nor did I even wince when Messer Pierettore denounced it by the epithet Childish, for now I was beyond concern for

---

[1] About £7,500, or $37,500.

[2] No doubt this was the edition issued in 1491.

these lesser matters, pondering the unmitigable calamity in which I stood.

Anon it was Ippolito's turn to do his lessons; and mine to amuse the guest. That one, by no means satisfied with the grave conversation of the cardinal, looked upon me as being a more suitable companion ; and he instantly proposed that we should ride through the City to see the sights of the night. I was by no means loath to oblige him : indeed the peril of such an adventure recommended itself to me as a means of escape from my melancholy.

While my decurion and the prince's were being collected, I chose my mail-shirt from a trayful. Ippolito had obtained a few minutes' interval in which to speed our departure ; and he praised my caution to Prince Gioffredo, saying that foolhardiness was not courage, and that vanity (however just) should not breed rashness. The Paparch's son watched me glittering in the pliant steel, while I was buckling-on my sword-belt ; and he said that I was as comely in the mail falling in escallops round mine haunches as I was in silk or velvet. Thus he spoke; and, finding on the tray another mail-shirt so fine that his two hands plump, juicy with heat, completely covered it, he let my pages do it on him. Certainly he made a gallant show; and a mirror taught him that veiling the splendour of the body (in such a gleaming web) enhances the splendour of the limbs : which gave him great content.

We mounted in the first court; and gave the word to our *ij* decurions. The great gate yawned before us; and clanged behind us. With a pomp of *xx* torches, we clattered over Tiber by the double-bridge and the Island. The night was young. The City was still : for the Keltic army chiefly lay outside the Flaminian Gate and in the Region of Campo Marzo. We rode quietly, bidding our guards to follow us : for so the light of their torches made clear the way, and our eyes were not dazzled with the glare.

The Prince of Squillace said that he was going to amuse himself. I, desperate with the oppression of my misery, declared that I also would amuse myself, Great Ban or no Great Ban, safely or unsafely. I had my sword and my *x* men with their lieutenant; and I would risk something for the sake of a little amusement.

Gioffredo said that Rome was a dull city, not to be compared for gaiety with little cities like Naples or Ferrara, seeing that Colonna and Orsini had eaten all the baronage save Cesarini, which last house alone remained leal to our Lord the Paparch. One might cultivate the arts, quoth he: or plague the rebellious barons and their Keltic friends: or sit in the Apostolic Palace making and unmaking kings and continents. But these were dismal sports, quoth he.

Little vulgar boys might go and throw stones on Campo Vaccino,[1] in defiance of the Cardinal-Vicar's edict, quoth I.

Degenerates, quoth he, might go and gamble

---

[1] The waste land which occupied the side of the then unexcavated Forum.

with the white-faced cardinal, who certainly was the pink of fashion, but whose luck was too infernally good for younger sons.

We agreed that princes were much to be commiserated.

Formerly, quoth Gioffredo, much diversion had been gained by hunting Jews or Bargelli,[1] slicing off their noses, or other ways afflicting them : but now the Paparch prohibited these exercitations, using Himself very kindly to the accursed race which so feloniously had slaughtered our Divine Redeemer, and being determined to keep order in the City by means of the said Bargelli. Wherefore, quoth he, these things being so, and the Paparch's Sanctity being not only so good but also so loving and so dear that no one but a devil wilfully would offend Him, it behoved respectable princes to be at some pains in obeying Him.

I loved the boy for those words, o Prospero : for they showed that a good heart accompanied his handsome person and his lightly merry

---

[1] Alexander the Sixth's police.

temper. But I found no word to say; and mine unhappiness overwhelmed me. We both were silent. Anon we halted on the Square of Santangelo.

Gioffredo leaned across to me, slyly saying that we ought to seek legitimate adventures. I took fire at his words; and we rode on, through and through the Street of the Bear, peeping in the inns where foreigners lay: but we savoured no spice of adventure in the public resorts. At Saint John's of the Florentines, we agreed to prowl separately; and, taking each our decurion, we chose different roads. Gioffredo went by Banchi Vecchi. I tried Giulia Street.

All the shops of the archers and armourers were shut on Campo de' Fiore; and the eyes of the houses twinkled with no light. I avoided the Square of Catinari: for I could not bear to see the razed palace of our house there; and I halted under the Capitol at the foot of Toasted Beans Lane. I was drowning in the cold waters of unhappiness. I also was molested by the pangs of hunger: for study doth augment

the carnal appetite most wonderfully, and, at
that time, it was necessary also that I continually
should heap fuel on the furnace of the prime of
mine adolescence. I diverged at a right angle,
proceeding through a series of narrow streets,
and by the black bulk of Rotondo[1] in the
Region of Pigna, to the Square of Saint
Eustace : where I dismounted at the new
Falcon Inn. Ippolito had spoken of this place,
as being already famous for its grotesque
chambers and its antic viands ; and I wished to
see for myself, and to taste food similar to that
which had gratified mine illustrious forefathers :
for it seemed that such a diversion would enable
me to overcome the malignance of my stars.

The chamber, which I chose, was shaped like
an isoskelene triangle couped at the apex by a circular alcove about *iij* braccie[2] in diameter. The
door was in the base of the triangle. The
walls and roof and tiled floor were porphyry-
colour. The last was strewn with lemon
verbena, a most delicious odour, invigorating,

---

[1] The Pantheon. [2] 7 feet 8 inches.

F

passion-inspiring. The alcove was a couch of cushions. The shuttered windows concealed their blindness behind white and porphyry-coloured curtains. A rush-seated settle waited by a bronze table in the middle ; and a lamp of *vij* wicks smiled from overhead. While I demanded supper of the innkeeper, I dismissed my cap and cloak into the alcove, giving my sword leave to rest by the bench, washing mine hands and combing mine hair as though there was no such thing as wretchedness on this orb of earth.

He named a boiled owl farced with assafoetida, a roasted wild-boar with sweet sauce and pine-kernels, a bear's hams, and a baked porpentine. I chose the boar and the porpentine for my proper repast, with a measure of the black wine of Marino ; and I sent the bear's hams and *xj* measures of wine to my decurion, paying two double giulj[1] for the entertainment.

A sturdy Roman hob, in snowy linen with black hosen and leathern bellyband, brought

---

[1] The double giulio was worth (say) a florin, but had about four times the latter's purchasing value.

napery and the apparatus of the table. He came again with a dish on each hand, and the wine-flask's loose rush cover gripped in his strong white teeth. This time, a clean-limbed youngster accompanied him, precociously and grandly formed, having a wonderful freshness of complexion, short curly brown hair, and an expression of disgust in his frank eyes.

The eye is the mirror of the soul, o Prospero, and it is of *ij* kinds, *videlicet* the open eye and the shut eye. The open eye denoteth a soul which is ready, willing, able, to enter into unreserved communion with its peer : not abnegating its proper rights, but sharing the same, according to the precepts of nobility. The shut eye is that eye wherein a veil is drawn continually, or at will, before the true image of the soul. It appertaineth to those unfortunate persons who, either from poorness of spirit or from vileness, wish to conceal their souls in selfish solitude. Note this, o Prospero. My proper preference (like that of all White Men) is for the open eye ; and having seen this youngster, I knew that some benignant star had deigned to send me one with whom I was in sympathy ; and I addressed myself to wait for further manifestations.

The boy appeared to be clothed on his arms and his sides and the outsides of his legs : but he really was covered from throat to wrist and foot with a single garment of knitted wool, resembling a skin, myrtle-green with a wide central stripe of flesh-colour, very ingenious. He did table-service inaccurately and disdainfully. It was plain that he never had served, and that he was accustomed to be served. Not a word was said while I satiated mine hunger.

When I had performed the last lavation, I lay back on the bench, stretching out my legs at length ; and I formed a totally erroneous idea of the avocation of mine attendant. I did not speak : but only looked at him. He furiously blushed ; and his eyes flamed. . . .

The events of the next quarter-hour will be set forth in another history, which thou, o Prospero, wilt read when thou shalt have come to the age of *xv* years. . . .

Anon, having summoned my lieutenant, I declared my will to him. I would rescue these *ij* children, taking the lad behind my saddle : but he would take the girl behind his. The decurion was to close our rear ; and all was to be swiftly done.

So it was done. There were protests and outcries at the door, a fine affray, hard blows ; and I stung more than one with my sword. But, when we were free of the crowd, I changed pursuers into scramblers, by scattering the contents of my burse on the cobble-stones ; and so I escaped with my spoils.

We galloped through the Square of Navona in the Region of Parione ;[1] and, by the tortuous lanes of the Region of Ponte to Saint John's of the Florentines.

Straightly behind me balanced, hands on his haunches, the lad rode. Strange was that fierce spell of riding through the darkness of night.

---

[1] The fourteen districts of Rome were called " Regions."

VII

THE City was quiet on the other side of Tiber and where we halted : but, on our right hand, the Keltic camp, now blazing with torches, hummed like a swarm of wasps. My guards lighted their own torches from the lanthorn which hung before the image of Saint John at the street corner.

We went onward slowly, through Banchi Vecchi and by the Cenci Palace, in search of Gioffredo : whom we found near the fort of Pierleone,[1] much disordered in his habits, his hosen being full of dried peas of which his decurion was relieving him. Their laughter prevented my words for a time. Wherefore, giving favour to my tongue, I consigned the

---

[1] I suppose this to be the ruined Theatre of Marcellus which the Pierleone fortified in the eleventh century. It is now the Palazzo Savelli.

Keltic lad to one of my proper guards ; and, when anon Gioffredo had remounted, we *ij* rode on side by side.

He was very loquacious concerning his adventures in a Jew's house, which used to stand by St. George's of the Golden Sail and the arch of Janus, where certain Jewesses had been entertaining him. But, their father having returned unexpectedly from some nocturnal orgy, they had hidden Gioffredo in the pea-bin : from which uncomfortable abode he at length emerged, deeming the moment convenient for flight. But the said Jew, having found a strange sword, was on the watch ; and furiously withstood him. Gioffredo had only a poignard and a mail-shirt, the latter in his hand instead of on his body : but, nevertheless, he had bidden old Abraham to bethink himself, seeing that the said poignard had been used for carving pork. But the Jew had enraged himself the more ; and Gioffredo, having all his points untrussed and his hosen about his feet, was unable to run. Wherefore, taking the mail-shirt by the sleeves, he swinged at his opponent such a blow that he fell prone, over whom incontinently rolling, the Paparch's son contrived to get into the street. He had lost his sword and his boots ; and he had spoiled his garments: but his speech was so comical, and his occasional jerks (when the movement of his horse caused him to sit upon a forgotten pea) by degrees dismissed the severity with which I at first was inclined to treat him. And also I was no saint myself. So I said. And so we came in silence to the Fabrician Bridge.

Gioffredo affectionately inquired the cause of my silence, saying that thinking made one grow old.

To whom I responded, saying that I was unhappy, and that all these games appeared to be only vain and rather silly, seeing that there were many other worthier occupations for princes of our quality. But, remembering that Gioffredo was a guest, anon I changed my mood, lightly asking whether he would wend to Vatican.

He would not; but he demanded half of my bed for the night, commanding his decurion to bring a valise of new habits from Traspontina,[1] for him to don on the morrow. And so we entered the palace.

Some malignant star caused a misfortune at our entrance. The soldier, who had my Keltic lad on his horse's crupper, dismounted; and began to unbuckle the girth. Near by, *ij* pages had been fighting; and one was bewailing and letting drip a bleeding nose. The odour of the blood enraged the stallion, on whose bare back the Keltic lad was sitting sideways, waiting for orders. That one promptly flung his leg over; and, leaning forward, seized the bridle. Insued sudden dispersal of the crowd, wild galloping through the courtyards, sidelong sweepings and rushings, heavenward tossings, frantic plungings; but the rider sat erect, tense as young Bellerophon before Chimaira, gripped to his steed by thighs and knees. Indeed, it was a very grand spectacle.

---

[1] The palace of the Cardinal of Saint Mary's across the Bridge, by the Vatican. It was rented for the Borgia princes.

While we all were gazing, the noise disturbed Ippolito : who came bounding down the stair, as the furious beast dashed through the low arch beneath the hall. That cardinal instantly cast his cardinalature to the *iiij* winds, leaping and tearing at the bitt with his gigantic strength, muffling the stallion's head in his vermilion mantle, while the grooms ran up and hobbled the dire hooves.

Anon the Keltic lad dismounted; and stood before us, blushing, trembling, bright-eyed, brave, a slender supple figure, with articulations of most delicate distinction. His glance strayed toward the girl. She stood still where she had been placed at first. In admiring him, I forgot that I myself was miserable. Gioffredo's eyes began to goggle.

Ippolito looked from the stranger to me. Having whispered what was necessary to the one, I announced to the other Ippolito's condition of Most Illustrious Lord Cardinal-Δ. and Prince of Ferrara. The Keltic lad kneeled; and did obeisance to the sapphire.

Ippolito resumed his cardinalature, stiffly asking the lad to name himself.

That one responded, saying that he was the Vicomte Réné XVIIII Raoul Alain Gabriel Marie de Sainctrose, Vidame de Sainctrose, Sieur de Chastelmondesir ; and now, o Prospero, thou knowest how thy father, and thy god-father, and Renato's,[1] first became acquainted each with other.

We all were much astonished. Ippolito demanded more news. To whom the Vicomte de Sainctrose was pleased to say that his father had had two brothers, *videlicet* the Sieur Estienne who was father to the Damoiselle Estelle there present and cousin of the speaker, and the Sieur Guichart who was father to the Damoiseau Armand then absent but also cousin of the speaker. Further he said that his own father and mother long had lived in olympian

---

[1] This would be that magnanimous Renato, son of the Marcantonio here mentioned, of whom Dom Gheraldo Pinarj so deliciously has written in his journal.

mansions :[1] that his uncle Estienne had gone
by the same road at Michaelmas: that his uncle
Guichart, being then his warden and the girl's,
and wishing to have his demesne and hers for
his own son, kept them both hardly, fearing by
cause that they loved one another. Wherefore,
on the day of the dead,[2] those *ij* had prayed
to their parents with the gods, and anon
escaped into the forest belonging to the said
Vicomte de Sainctrose, intending to love and to
die there. But a company of Egyptians had
captured them; and had brought them, with
other stolen children, by long roads to the City,
selling them as slaves.

Ippolito interrupted, saying something about
an evil trade.

The Vicomte indignantly gainsaid him: as-
severating that he himself and his cousin had
been but a night and a day in the City; and
that, as he was not alone, it behoved him to use

---

[1] A pretty way of saying that they were gone to
heaven.

[2] All Souls' Day, the second of November.

subtilty for the sake of his said cousin. He denied that he had followed an evil trade, having a knife, which either would cause force to flee, or would open Paradise for the girl and for him then speaking.

Ippolito still demurred: but Réné persisted, saying:

"The Most Illustrious Prince Tarquinio Giorgio Drakontoletes Poplicola di Hagio-stayros used princely words and kindlike, the first from strangers during many months: for which cause We wished to let him know that a Keltic noble could be as generous as a Roman patrician."

And he added, in the Greek tongue, that he venerated me as his Deliverer.[1]

As thou well knowst, o Prospero, the road to my love lieth through Hellas; and, when I heard that last word of the Vicomte de Sainctrose, my bowels yearned because of him.[2]   I said:

---

[1] ἐλευθερωτης.

[2] Don Tarquinio was a great one for judging by the evidence of his senses. The brave and pitiful little

" Tell us thine age, o Damoiseau."

He responded to me, saying that the nones of April would mark the opening of his fifteenth year.

When I understood that he had been born under the Ram and Mars, the cause of his extraordinary courage and of the astounding manner in which he had governed his affairs, at once became clear to me. Desiring to be asso-

---

vicomte had told an amazing tale ; and there was not a shred of corroborative detail. If this had happened in the nineteenth century, they of course would have interned the couple in more or less criminal seclusion, until they had obtained a pack of identificatory papers— which any fool can forge. But it luckily happened in the fifteenth century, when men (being men of sense) believed in God, Who had made them in His Own Image ; and, consequently, they felt no false delicacy about assuming for themselves some of the divine attributes—for example, the power of recognizing truth when they saw and heard it. Prince Tarquinio heard the Vicomte de Sainctrose : he looked into his open eyes ; and decided that the thing was true—saving himself (and everyone else) an infinity of trouble by his sensibility.

ciated with such an one, I completed my deliberations with these words:

"We offer to take thee into Our service."

He responded to me again, saying that he desired nothing better than to learn the duties of his estate, in order that he might oust the usurper of his feoffs at an opportune time. But his eyes wandered to the girl.

I said that the comptroller should have order regarding him, and that the mistress of the women should have order regarding the damoiselle: for, being no more than a guest in the Estense palace, I was in a quandary at the moment. And so I turned away, with Ippolito and the Borgia boy. As we went, I was telling Ippolito more of what had happened at the Falcon Inn. Gioffredo continually ejaculated concerning the good fortune of certain people: but Ippolito's brow became as black as night. Anon he interrupted me; and took command of the whole matter, saying that he would not know of any sin or of anything needing amendment in his palace. And he began to act.

The page Giovempedocle (he was very finely made, o Prospero, but his right eye was brown while his left eye was blue) evanesced with an order for the mistress of the women to conduct the Damoiselle Estelle de Sainctrose to the cedar cabinet with a vicecomitial escort.

The page Giacinto (he was quite young, but his hair was as white as hoar-frost and very luxuriant indeed) evanesced with an order for an abbate (whose name I have forgotten) to attend in the chapei.

But we returned ; and joined the Vicomte de Sainctrose to our company. Réné was palpitating with emotions not necessary to be described. I took his hand ; and we followed Ippolito to the treasury, where a choice was made of certain matters. As we went along, a full state of gentlemen and chamberlains with the double-cross collected ; and attended us to the cedar cabinet.

There, we withdrew the *ij* Keltic nobles to the window, where we could speak in secret ; and Ippolito examined them as to their real

sentiments each for other. Their wonderful
frank eyes became grave as they responded,
saying that they were one. He gave rings
to them, each ring a flight of golden cupids
bound with scrolls inscribed 𝕵𝖊 𝖘𝖛𝖎' 𝖎𝖈𝖎 𝖊𝖓 𝖑𝖎'𝖛
𝖉' 𝖆𝖒𝖕 and 𝕱𝖎𝖑𝖟 𝖔𝖛 𝕱𝖎𝖑𝖑𝖊. Taking their
hands, he led them to the chapel. The presbyter
blessed the rings. They were exchanged and
planted. Benediction hallowed nuptials, legitimate, indissoluble.

Thus was one of the many grand deeds
done by thy father, o my son Prospero, well
done on that fortunate day.

G

VIII

WE conducted the bridegroom and his bride
to an apartment on the second stair ; and the
door was shut. Ippolito returned to his
lessons : but I took Gioffredo to my proper
lodging.

Having seen those children happy, I felt
mine own unhappiness surging again in my
breast. By the grace of the gods, the Borgia
boy chattered like a pie all the time, enraptured
with his own garrulity, needing no attention.
Thus I was able to let my proper thoughts
range freely. We rested in arm-chairs, while
the pages doffed our garments, wrapping us in
white woollen frocks.

It was not to be denied that I had done a
noble deed in rescuing those children from
a den of infamy. I looked at the sheets,
filled with fragrant herbs, which hung by their

corners from the ceiling of the bathing-chamber, as though I expected a message of approval from the Divine Ones who live in that direction. We were sitting on large sponges placed on rush-seated stools upon the floor-sheet ; and pages laid other sponges under our feet.

I remember noting that Gioffredo's big toes were his longest toes : but my second toes are my longest toes, according to the canon of Lysippos.[1] Otherwise his form was without blemish ; and if, as Ippolito alleged, I in mine adolescence resembled the marble copy of the lithe thalerose image of David by Messer Verrocchio, certainly the Borgia boy at that time

---

[1] This would be the Athlete with the Strigil, the Apoxyomenos, the supreme model of human form, which is so unaccountably and yet so assiduously neglected by all "strong men" and physiculturists of the present day. It is strange that this statue should be named by Don Tarquinio : for it was not discovered till A.D. 1849, though it certainly was discovered in Trastevere, the district of Rome in which Don Tarquinio was in A.D. 1495.

resembled the sleek plump image of David by Messer Donatello, which images copied in tinted marble the white-faced cardinal then possessed. So I judged ; and I resolved to mention this particular to Ippolito : not that I actually believed myself to resemble the beautiful Rufo Drudo-dimare, admirable, pathetic, or Gioffredo to resemble the splendid Baldonero Fioravanti, admirable, treacherous, in more particulars than a few and those very superficial : but those *ij* adolescents had been mistaken for the very images themselves above-named ; and so we *ij* also possessed a certain similitude to the same, but only to the casual spectator. However, the thing was strange ; and I pondered it in my mind.

Anon I began to wonder what colour of body his stars had deigned to Réné. That his form was as exquisite and as vigorous as his mind, I already knew from the evidence of my sense of sight : but I often have noted that a fine form and fine features sometimes are marred by some imperfect tincture of the skin in parts; and I eagerly looked forward to the morrow, when I might take an opportunity of assuring myself as to the person of one whose individuality seemed to be so sympathetic.

After these rather absurd meditations, I went on to consider the likely effects of my deed of the night.

The pages had placed beneath our stools great silver bowls containing the steaming stew of hollyhock, mallow, pellitory, sweet fennel, wall-wort, johnswort, centaury, rib-grass, camomile, heyhove, heyriff, herbbenet, daisy, wild-water-parsley, water-speedwell, scabious, henbane, withy-leaves, green oats, all boiled to a pulp in distilled water. Note the composition of this bath, o Prospero. It was invented by one of his mages for the cardinal; and as conducing to physical health, it hath no equal. I heard the senior page reciting the names of the herbs, as I had heard him on the *vij* previous nights, while the others wrapped us and our stools closely in thick woollen cloths

of enormous size.   While thus we sat sweating
in the odoriferous steam, Gioffredo incessantly
gabbled : but I cogitated many things in my
mind.

It appeared to me that I had delivered a
Keltic noble from slavery, had enabled him
to provide himself with legitimate heirs of his
body in contempt of his wicked uncle, and that
I was going to enable him sooner or later to
achieve his natural rights and dignities.   In
plain words, I had laid him under a debt of
gratitude.   Secondly, I had conceived an
immense affection for him, which he in turn
seemed to reciprocate.   In plain words, I
had acquired another friend who might be
valuable.

At this point of the argument, the cloths
were removed ; and our flesh was seen to be
as scarlet as the flesh of tunny-fish.   The pages
sponged us with tepid rose-water ; and several
bucketfuls of cold, poured over our heads when
we stood up, caused pallor anon to conquer
ruddiness.   So we stood on dry sheets by the

glow of the fire, spitting into gold basins while cleaning our teeth with linen, moistened in a liquid made of mastic, rosemary, sage, bramble-leaves all macerate in Greek wine, and dipped in a powder of barley-bread burned with salt. This was the recipe which our mage of Deira gave to me ; and I gave it to Ippolito.

The pages dried our bodies, chafing our limbs with their hands ; but I was persuading myself that such a friend as the Vicomte de Sainctrose might be very useful to me anon, supposing that Ippolito should fail to induce our Lord the Paparch to treat me fairly : for, I deliberated, if the Great Ban were to continue in force against me here, I should be compelled to seek an opportunity for expending mine energies else-where. And I stretched myself, looking down upon my tremendous natural capabilities with anger at the thought that they were totally use-less. I most earnestly desired to sting someone.

Gioffredo went on chattering. I believe that he had not found me a good listener : for he was addressing himself to the pages who were rubbing his ribs. We went into the bed-chamber for the drying and combing of our hair. Long before this was finished, Gioffredo slept where he sat in his chair. The service was a poor one for the son of our Lord the Paparch, accustomed to luxuries as he was: but he himself had chosen his lot, and his breeding prohibited complaint.

But I, on my part, bitterly complained of evil knitting in the hosen which I had doffed, re-ducing my comptroller to terror, very comical, lest he should be degraded from his situation; for mine anger at the malignance of my stars made me angry with all and singular. What was the use, I reflected, of a Keltic friend, not *xv* years old, dispossessed of his demesnes, and actually dependent on me for a livelihood? And I thought bitterly of Réné blissfully mounted and riding to fortune, and of myself writhing under the oppression of the Great Ban.

Our hair having been tucked into our night-caps, nothing now remained but that we should betake ourselves to bed. But, while the pages were spreading the footcloths, and covering the rush-lights with shades, and opening the windows, Gioffredo suddenly awakened and would have been merry. I myself was in no mood for sleep: nor could I join in his mirth. But I suggested that we *ij* should go to find Ippolito.

A couple of my best nightgowns[1] were brought; and the Borgia boy chose the one of vair of nut-brown squirrels, with slippers of the same: but I indued the other of ermine reversed with ermines, with slippers of minever. I remember this, by cause that both these nightgowns were of great value, and after this night I never saw either of them again.[2]

---

[1] He means "dressing-gowns," I surmise: for gentlemen of the fifteenth century slept as God made them.

[2] It's extremely likely. They appear to have been cast off in a great hurry a little later, in a place accessible to many miscellaneous persons. Patricians, who fling away fur nightgowns among people not responsible for their preservation, ought not to be surprized when they lose them. Valuable fur nightgowns are saleable; and—strange, but absolutely true, to say—

Thus we proceeded ; and we found the cardinal writing, in the secret chamber, still engaged with his tasks.

Rome was full of Jews who had fled from Torquemada and the Spanish Inquisition to the generous protection of Pope Alexander the Sixth.

VIIII

WHILE we washed our fingers on entering, Ippolito threw aside his writing, making room for us on the big black heap of cushions. He was too grand a prince to be a bad host.

As soon as the servitors were gone, Gioffredo began again to recite his adventures with much noise and gesture. I let him talk; and sat a little apart, in silence, thinking my proper thoughts, wishing for the time when I might consult Ippolito thereon. A twice-told tale is not always very amusing: but the Borgia boy gabbled so insistently and so incessantly that I at last was compelled to listen. I will not set down his words: for they were of no importance whatever, but merely as bright and as sharp and as pleasant and also as ephemeral as the foam of the sea. He omitted no singular particular of his exploits. Had the matter been an Easter shrift, it could not have been more explicit. He was exquisitely droll, frankly shameless.

Ippolito gradually lapsed into gloom : a species of distaste affected him. But I, for want of something better, began to be amused. The thing was infectious. And anon, when I also began to speak in the same strain, the cardinal revolted against us both, crying :

" Is woman all ? Is there naught else in Total Christendom to serve you in passing time? Thou, o Prince of Squillace, hast tried war : men name thee fearless. It can be seen that thou hast lively wits as well as robust sinews. Canst thou not use these for Madonna Sancia thy wife, or for thy Most Holy Father in His need, leaving vulgar adventures to pages or apprentices? And thou, o Sideynes, hast hyperexcellent parts. We never have seen an adolescent more godlike in white splendour of body and mind, though thou knowest that We keep *xl* merchants travelling over the orb of the earth solely to seek and to purchase for Us

such monstrosities. There is not a man, there
is not a sovereign, equal to thee in birth.
Th' art healthy, strong. With the sword thou
hast not a peer : also, Messeri Claudio and
Pierettore Arrivabene both say that thy written
Greek might be the Greek of an archangel.
And they should know, having been the friends
of the Divine Poliziano, on whom be peace. It
is true that We could kill thee with one hand.
Domeniddio so made Us : putting into these
limbs that which, after mature consideration,
He might have put into Our head. Different
calamities oppress different persons.[1] Of ad-
vantages also each hath his own : to Us, Our
purple and Our strength of body : to the
Prince of Squillace, lusty sinews and a daring
mind and an opportunity : to thee, o Sideynes,
splendid wits, adolescence full of grace, and the
aspect of one nourished on the marrow and

---

[1] συμφορα ετερους ετερα πιεζει (Eyripides). These
conversations are interesting, as showing the taste of
the times for displaying acquaintance with the Greek
writers, if on no other account.

nerves of lions. And ye *ij* are content to squander these gifts on women."

Thus he spoke; and the speech was a very memorable one. The sudden outburst and the pungent force of it set me striding to and fro, with my fists clenched and my brows drawn straight to the upright furrow above dilated eyes, sea-blue, glittering. And now my mind was in a whirl: for I knew that this was my chance for speaking unwinged words, which should lie and germinate and bear fruit there where I flung them. I could not ask for boons. I could not propose plans. But, with certain furious selected speeches, I might disclose the intimate root of mine unhappiness, of my despair.

But Gioffredo instantly had taken him up, saying:

"Where is Our opportunity, o prudent Purpled Person? Give Us Our Sancia; and she shall swoon with joy. Give Us Our free-lances; and We will lead them against devils. But, when there is neither wife nor war for Us,

when Sancia is yet in the straw, and the Keltic
army is about to take flight, and our Most
Holy Father sitteth silent and solemn in the
Castle, what else can We do but accept such
adventures as We find ?"

But I stopped in my fierce striding; and
inveighed, saying :

"Hear Us also, o Hebe, Us, thy Sideynes,
descended from Zeys not only on the spade
but also on the distaff side.[1] Thou well
knowst how We are : Our house being under
the Great Ban, Our palace razed, Our princes
bandits, Madonno Marcantonio a meek student
in exile, Madonno Francesco in exile with a
price upon his head, Madonno Giorgio in exile
hunted for his life since he slew Colonna.
Why should We not amuse Ourself with the
Prince of Squillace, seeing that no better way
lieth open to Us ? Why dost thou decry
such pleasures, when thine own hero Herakles

---

[1] ὀυ μονον προς πατρος ἀλλα και προς μητρος
ἀπο Διος γεγονοτες (Isokrates).

married the most women that ever one man did?[1] Know that Our adolescence burneth like a furnace *vij* times heated. It must have vent. Where can we vent it? We are tolerated in this place only by cause of thy protection and of Our Own insignificance. What advantage is life to Us?[2] What chance of a career have We?"

Ippolito threw up his grand head; and sturdily injuncted, saying:

"Make a career with that thine intellect, o dear Sideynes. Where the will is, there will be a way.[3] In spite of thy words, thou knowst that the pleasures of sense are inferior to the pleasures of the intellect. Let thy mind be thy ruler and governour. As Messer Lionardo[4] saith, Make thine own life as thou wouldst make any other work of art: the life

---

[1] πλειστας ανηρ εἰς Ἡρακλης ἐγημε δη (Sophokles).

[2] τι μοι ζην κυδιον (Eyripides).

[3] θαρσει παρεσται μηχανη δραστηριος (Aischylos).

[4] This is Lionardo da Vinci.

of intellect should be of intellect's own design :
to have but not to be had,[1] is the rule from
which intellect must not swerve. Further,
trust in thy splendid stars ; and take no
count of Fortune, whose name is not in any
martyrologium.[2] She hath, indeed, no Divine
Creator, for any man may make her at his
will : of whom Messer Decimus Junius Juve-
nalis hath written, Thou, o Fortune, art not
divine where prudence is, for it is we, we,
who make thee a goddess and place thee in
heaven.[3] Why dost thou pause to play the
fool ? By cause that thou art not free to
work out thine own salvation ? So. Now
mark me well and closely, o Sideynes. Be
it known to thee that Alexander, magnificent,
invincible, loveth beauty, loveth wit ; and

---

[1] Habere non haberi.

[2] The Roman Martyrology is the official roll of
sanctity.

[3] Nullum numen habes, si sit prudentia : nos te,
nos facimus, Fortuna, deam ; cœloque locamus.

(Satura X.)

those twain in one person need not lack His
favour for a paltry disability, such as the
Great Ban. Wilt thou serve Him with thy
body, with thy mind? With the last, thou
wilt have a chance of shewing thy goodness.[1]
Know also that on the morrow We ride to
Vatican, where We shall render a certain
account. This done, it will be Our privilege
to demand a boon. Thou wilt go with Us,
o Sideynes?"

Gioffredo wagged a long leg, plump, carna-
tion-coloured, out of his brown fur nightgown;
and yelped, saying:

"No, no, go not, o Tarquinio: for Our
Most Holy Father starveth Himself and His
guests. But We and thou will ride to Vatican
with the lord cardinal; and there part peace-
fully. He will proceed by Lo Andare to
render his said account: but we *ij* will cross
to Our palace of Traspontina, where food is,

---

[1] κιιδυνευσεις ἐπιδειξαι χρηστος ἐιναι (Xeno-
phon).

and wine, and many maids-of-honour to be tickled."

Ippolito angrily ejaculated :

" Women again !"

To whom the pert prince responded, saying :

" But only for passing the afternoon pleasantly, which is the point of Our argument."

The noble strong young cardinal gravely said:

" Thy Venus We totally disregard.[1] The point of the whole argument is the salvation of Our well-beloved friend, Prince Tarquinio."

Thus he spoke ; and it was enough. I kneeled to him, kissing his sapphire, and saying :

" We accede to the Lord Cardinal of Ferrara :[2] for thou, o Hebe, art not only grand

---

[1] την σην δε Κυπριν πολλ' ἐγω χαιρειν λεγω (Eyripides).

[2] This is a witty misuse of the formula employed in the Conclave, when cardinals elect the Paparch by the way of accession after the way of scrutiny has failed.

but also good. Nevertheless We will not dine with our Lord the Paparch: for food, and food in bulk, We must have lest Our wits wither and Our sinews shrivel. Neither will We consent to ask a favour, nor to accept thy mediation: but We will that Alexander, magnificent, invincible, should see Us as We shall shew Ourself to Him, and that He should hear Us as it were by accident. If that can be contrived, well. If not, let Us have a chance of serving Him, so that We may compel Him to deal fairly by Us. If neither of these things can be done now, bear them in mind. Now that thou knowst Our desire, We are content to wait patiently for some benignant affection of Our stars; and We no more will meddle with base matters."

Thus I spoke: for the genuine loving-kindness of Ippolito cheered me. I knew not, at that moment, anything save that I was happier in my mind; and, being at length desirous of turning the conversation away from myself, I continued, saying:

"But tell Us, o Hebe, hast thou never amused thyself as we *ij* have been amusing ourselves? Sometimes We have thought."

Ippolito instantly demanded:

"What hast thou thought?"

I responded to him, saying:

"That thou at some time hast been like the rest of us, loving a woman: that thou hast lost her, and cherish but the wreck of thy love."

He smiled; and his whole being seemed to open, blossoming like a rose. He, with full breath, said:

"We have loved: but We have had no lover; and We very greatly love."

Gioffredo gabbled:

"Oh, oh, oh! And whom? Madonna Lucrezia? Yes: so it must be: for all men love Our sister."

Ippolito said:

"Nay. Our lady is of Gaul, not of Spain."

We both stammered:

"Of Gaul?"

We gritted our teeth : for the saying was a terrible one, akin to treachery.

Ippolito proclaimed, with tremendous magnificent unfolding :

"She is the unique illumination which hath lighted Gaul, and through all ages still shall light that land from the throne where she sitteth beyond the stars."

We waited : for the moment was one of revelation.

His great black eyes became deliberate and grave. He continued, saying :

"Our Lord Alexander Himself made Us to know her *ij* years ago. The Holiness of Him saw Us to be lusty and froward, unworthy of the purple which Our father Duke Ercole sent Us to have of Him. Wherefore He questioned Us concerning Our loves ; and, finding that insatiate desire and strenuous strife had failed to cheer, He told Us, oh but gently, as we walked in the court under the Borgia Tower,——(the cardinal was speaking, o my Prospero, of the court where the

Paparch Julius placed the image of that mediocre anisopod which He called the Apollo of the Belvedere[1])——He told Us of a maid so sympathetic that the mere name of her put Our heart in chains. She was well-grown, strong-limbed, young, of the age of *xvij* years, He said. Her land was distracted by more than a century of years of war. Her sovereign was a slave. Came to her for strength, the god Michael Archangel : came to her for wisdom and for maiden charm, the goddesses Katharine and Margaret, all in an orchard of apple-bloom. These divine ones brought word that she must go to save her fatherland and to crown her king. Many times they came. And she went. She gave news that she was of divine sending ; and

---

[1] " Anisopode mediocre " in the original holograph. "The Unequal-legged one," or "The Limper," is an exquisite name for that silly, stupid, utterly vulgar caricature of Phoibos Apollōn, the Bright, the Pure, which the nineteenth century regarded as a work of art.

shewed tokens. That little girl commanded armies, strove with sword, took blows and gave. In *ij* years, she brought to her country that deliverance which men had failed to compass in an hundred. Her crowned king ennobled her : she had given him the means. But anon she was captured treacherously by the flying foe : they traded her to foes of her own country who of envy sought her life. The chief of these last, and he was a bishop, bought her : fraudulently adjudged her Heretic, Heretic by cause that she was urged by heavenly voices, fraudulently by cause that she stated an appeal to God's Vicegerent here on earth, thus soaring far above merely episcopal jurisdiction. But that foul prelate had might. The girl had only right. And he was promised an archbishopric for her death. He suppressed her appeal. He laid the Great Ban on her. She most miserably died for a most glorious deed :[1]

---

[1] κακιστ' ἀπ' ἐργων εὐκλεεστατων φθινει (Sophokles).

for he afflicted her with natural death by fire.
Wait. Her king who owed her a crown,
her countrymen who owed her their liberty,
were craven cowards having the bowels and
brains of apes from Barbary. They minced
and gibbered and grimaced ; and they let her
burn. They were Keltic dogs. What could
ye expect? But, after *xx* years, that Christian
King[1] found that he held his crown from a
girl whom Holy Church (ill-served by that
satanic bishop) had burned as bandit and
heretic ; and for his crown he trembled most
exceedingly. Wherefore, after those *xx* years,
he let Rome have that holy maid's appeal.
Our Lord the Paparch all incontinently pre-
conized new judges, who, having examined
the whole case, pronounced her to be all that
they would desire their own sisters to be,
videlicet holy, maiden, favourite and ambas-
sador of Divine Ones inhabiting olympian
mansions. This their decree was confirmed

---

[1] " The Christian King " is the official style of the
Kings of France.

in form. That marvel, that miracle, that adorable sweet child, that most courageous palatine, Madame Jehane de Lys by her king's creation, called The Maid by Christendom, so foully killed and slain, was named by God's Vicegerent as one of the blessed carrying lilies in paradise, wearing an immortal diadem. She is the lady of Our love and worship. As ivy clingeth to oak, so will We cling to her memory. It was the Lord Alexander who made us to know her, as We have said. He Himself had her history when, in His Own youth, He entered the Sacred College with that self-same Bishop of Constance, Archpresbyter of the Vatican basilica, the Lord Richart de Longvevil Olivier, Cardinal-presbyter of the Title of Santa Susanna, who had been one of the judges of the Maid. Moreover, ye shall know that it was the said Lord Alexander's Own uncle and creator, the Paparch Calixtus the Third, Who decreed her rehabilitation."

Thus Ippolito spoke: but we bestowed

favour on our tongues, revolving the whole matter in our minds.

Sitting erect on the black cushions, he murmured these words in an undertone :

" Saincte Vierge et Martyre, dictée Jehane d' Arcques, priez toulzjours pour moy et pour toulz tes serviteurs."

Gioffredo eyed him, decorously waiting for licence to speak. I was hugging mine own bare arms in the sleeves of my nightgown ; and my glance was directed to the toes of my slippers which were stretched out straight together in front of me.

But my mind was wandering far away to a live love, yearning for her who was sleeping over there in the dark.

X

But our meditations were interrupted by an instant scratching on the outside of the ivory door ; and a wave of secret chamberlains flowed in with torches, announcing :

"The Most Respectable Worship[1] of the Lord Cardinal of Valencia."

Ippolito arose, grave, self-dominant. I and Gioffredo also arose, wrapping our furs more closely round us, surprized, very greatly wondering.

I will tell thee, o Prospero, how Cardinal Cesare appeared to me on that night : so that

---

[1] Cesare (whom the nineteenth century was apt to call "Borgia") ranked as a pontifical nephew : hence his proper epithets were "Osservantissimo" and "Colendissimo." The other cardinals were "Illustrissimo." The style "Most Eminent" and "Eminency" was not invented in 1495.

thou mayst have ever before thine eyes a vivid image of the prodigious personality who, as Messer Niccolo Machiavelli saith, might have done Anything. He was of the age of *xx* years, tall and splendid of form. Tawny hair and beardlet shaded his swarthy features. The hair was rolled in a golden bag of network convenient for travelling. His eyes were like glowing iron in the furnace of his face. Under the cardinalitial great-cloak, he wore a secular habit of vermilion velvet. The huge sapphire[1] glittered on the first finger of his right hand. A thick gold chain surrounded his neck, disappearing in the lace of the smock which peeped out of the breast of his doublet. Beneath the lower hem of the last, the escalloped edge of a mail-shirt appeared. All this I noted, while he was washing his fingers at the door.

His pages caught the great-cloak flung to them : left the double-cross leaning against one

---

[1] The sapphire is the proper stone for a cardinal's ring, as the amethyst is for a bishop's or an archbishop's.

of the ivory images ; and retired ; and the door was shut. He advanced towards the Cardinal of Ferrara : but he was winking at Gioffredo with haggard brilliant eyes. As for me, he noted me no more than the said ivory images : whereat I fumed with rage, only restraining myself from using my sting by cause that I desired to see more of this splendid creature.

Ippolito accorded to him the kiss of peace : to whom he spoke, saying :

" In virtue of his obedience to our Lord the Paparch, We are to demand secret conference with the Cardinal of Ferrara."

It was evident from the form of this speech that very great matters were afoot. I instantly shot such a glance at Ippolito as taught him my vehement desire to be mixed up with the affair. Such was the force of my will that the thing was understood as readily as though I had spoken.

Ippolito went to the door ; and issued commandments to the chamberlains in the antechamber.

Cardinal Cesare was pinching the plump legs of Gioffredo in a merry manner, running round the room.

Anon a guard of *viiij* gigantic Numidians, ebony-coloured, girt with jaguar-skins, white and tawny, armed with terrible clubs, produced themselves; and were ranged outside, in a wedge whose base was the ivory portal. But *xviij* other Numidians in the outer ante-chamber kept the way against all comers. And so the door again was shut.

Ippolito beckoned me to him; and placed me with my back against it, making it my charge. I kept silence: but my looks told him of my gratitude.

Gioffredo escaped from his tormentor; and taking the comb from his pouch, tidied his ruffled hair, and resumed his nightcap.

Ippolito and the Cardinal of Valencia disposed themselves on the black cushions. The former drew up the low ivory tables of wine and sweetmeats, beginning to chew fresh sage-leaves from a vase: but the latter degusted

spoonfuls of a confection of prickly pear. Anon
Gioffredo joined himself to them. But I
munched coriander-seeds steeped in marjoram-
vinegar and crusted with sugar, which by
chance I had in my comfit-box. They bring a
special commodity to the memory, o Prospero.

Cesare abruptly asked Ippolito how much he
knew of affairs.

Ippolito responded, saying that he very
assiduously had been playing at great-ball since
his return to the City, and had not paid
much attention to affairs. He knew, of course,
that Alexander, magnificent, invincible, had
interned Himself in the castle ; and that the
Keltic king was occupying part of the City on
the other side of Tiber. Also he knew, from
rumour, that the said king's nose resembled a
raw ham, that a pink birth-flare surrounded
his left eye, that his twelve-toed shanks had no
more form than women's spindles, that he had
brought into the City a new disease which he
who was speaking called Morbus Gallicus, but
Prince Tarquinio here present called it Morbus

Kelticus, and the Cardinal of Valencia might decide between us. Finally, resuming his gravity, Ippolito named the rumour which said that the said Keltic king, finding our Lord the Paparch to be quite impregnable, was forced to conclude some sort of peace.

Cesare silently produced the pectoral cross which was attached to his neck-chain. It was set with great table-rubies. Unfastening its clasp, he disengaged a ring, huge, massive, which hung by its side. I never had seen so enormous a ring then. It was made of gilded bronze, *viiij* barleycorns in diameter. Its oblong bezel was set with a cabochon rock-crystal, highly projecting. One shoulder was carved with the Borgia armorials, *videlicet* Sol a Bull passant Mars on a closet Venus flory proper within a bordure Mars semée of flammels Sol.[1] The Triple Crown and the Keys were carved on the other shoulder. The

---

[1] The tinctures are given by Don Tarquinio as in the arms of princes. Sol = or, Mars = gules, Venus = vert.

I

legend **papa aler bi** was carved on the hoop. This ring, as thou knowst, o Prospero, is the most precious thing in my proper treasury at the time of writing : for which cause I am able to describe it, although at the time of which I write I was not able to see more than its tremendous magnitude and its reddish colour.

While he was disentangling this ponderous jewel, Cesare was cursing in the urbane and simple manner of a real Roman of Rome, saying :

" That a Worship of my Respectability should be compelled to carry so vulgar an ingot, a sordid lump only intended for couriers to wave at post-houses in passing by, a blasted gyve which even a blind postmaster could not fail to see !"

With which words he presented the said ring to the Cardinal of Ferrara.

Ippolito kneeled, applying his ear to it with surprise and reverence,[1] ejaculating :

---

[1] This would appear to be the Roman method of answering an official citation—as old as Horace, anyhow.

" Credentials ?"

Cesare assented :

" Credentials on the part of our Most Holy Father."

Ippolito maliciously inquired :

" Father ?"

Cesare jumped up ; and put himself to stride about the room. At first he shouted : but anon his voice sank into the tone of self-communion ; and finally, resuming his seat, he returned to an ordinary mode of speech. He said :

" Father? Yes, father. Pater patrum. Thine as well as Ours. Oh We catch the sneer of thy meaning, o Cardinal of Ferrara. But We mean Father after the spirit. Whether after the flesh also, who knoweth? Not We, for one. He is generous to Us : but He is not fatherlike to Us. Nor do We Ourself believe —no, We do not believe. There be secret mysteries, incongruities. Yet We dare not ask her. But she was the other's before she was His. And the time of Our birth coincideth.

Did We ever tell thee, o Cardinal of Ferrara of the woman who screamed at Us out of the crowd at Naples when We took Gioffredo to his marriage? See the Dellarovere, she cried, wagging a stark finger at Us. But enough. Thou takest cognizance of this Our credentials?"

Remember, o Prospero, that thy father heard those pregnant words, while his eyes saw that splendid creature laying bare his mind. So thou shalt know truly who was the actual father of Cesare whom men called Borgia.

He put the great ring on his right middle finger.

Ippolito again offered his ear to be touched by the ring; and responded, saying:

"We recognize; and We are ready to obey."

Cesare began to deliver his message, saying:

"Then listen: for time is short. Thou knowest nothing of affairs. Well, We will treat thee honestly. Always We save Ourself

pains so. First, thou shalt know that the
Christian King, on pretence of a crusade
against the Grand Turk, obtained leave from our
Lord the Paparch to march his troops through
Italy. On the way, he conceived a claim to the
crowns of Aragon, Naples, Both Sicilies, and
Hierusalem. At Fiorenza, he intrigued with
the maniac Fra Girolamo,[1] whose proper place
should be Santo Spirito.[2] When anon the said
Christian King reached the City, finding himself with an army at his back, he dared to
require our said Lord the Paparch to confirm
his claim, knowing that (without such recognition) he can wear no crown. But Alexander,
magnificent, invincible, having no particular
grievance against King Don Alonzo of Naples
and the rest, who already is in possession,
refused to depose that sovereign in favour of
the Christian King. Wherefore that Keltic
monkey, in revenge, conspired with the traitor
Cardinal-bishop Giuliano Dellarovere, and with

---

[1] This would be Savonarola.
[2] The Roman "Bedlam."

his friends the traitor barons Colonna, Orsini, Savelli, Sanseverini, Cajetani; and he even hath won the Cardinal-vicechancellor Sforza-Visconti with Cardinal-presbyter Sanseverini and Cardinal-Δ. Lunati. Then he appealed to the arbitrement of war. What cared the invincible Alexander? Having laid hands on those *iij* treacherous purpled persons, He nipped them in the dungeons of the castle. Taking the Sultán Jam[1] along with Him, He Himself also retired into the castle, snapping a thumb and finger at the Christian King."

Ippolito interrupted, demanding the reason for the sequestration of the said Sultán Jam.

To whom Cesare responded, saying:

"The Sultán Jam is of inestimable value to our Lord the Paparch, by cause that he is the brother and rival of the Grand Turk. The said potentate, by name the Sultán Bajazet, preferreth not to be dethroned by the Sultán

---

[1] This Oriental personage appears to have been somewhat of a Man-in-the-Iron-Mask in the Borgian Era.

Jam. Wherefore he agreed to pay *xlm* ducats yearly to the Supreme Pontiff, so long as that He shall keep the said brother and rival from Byzantion. Lately no ducats have been paid ; and the Grand Turk now demandeth the person of the Sultán Jam. But the Sanctity of the Paparch knoweth *ij* things. First, that the Sultán Bajazet hath a mind to kill and slay his brother ; and the magnificent Alexander will not become a proximate occasion of fratricide. Secondly, that so long as that Christian hands retain the Sultán Jam, so long will the Muslim Infidel refrain from advancing nefariously on Hungary and Vienna, lest Christendom, postponing private quarrels, should combine to set up the Sultán Jam in his despite, having obtained warranties of good behaviour. Wherefore, although the said Sultán Jam actually is our pensioner, our Lord the Paparch generously permitteth him to keep his own court here with Him in the security of the Castle of Santangelo."

Ippolito ejaculated :

"Good, good !¹ Either the Paparch's Blessedness or Thy Worship's Respectability, We know not which, is as expert and as artificial with the wits of the head as We are with the sinews of Our body."

Cesare continued, saying:

"These things having been understood, thou art to know that the Christian King made a show of siege, sitting down before the Castle of Santangelo with a gaggle of the common queans of the City and the stinking strumpets of the stews. But, after this diversion, he seeth that the paparchal fortress is too hard a nut to crack. As the Sieur de Commines confessed to Us, he hath become aware that the deposition of our Lord the Paparch is beyond his power. As Messer Demosthenes saith, The mouse hath found out that he is eating pitch.² And so the said Christian King will be wholly glad to go away, if he can save

---

¹ " ἐυγε, ἐυγε " in the original holograph.
² ᾽αρτι μυς γενεται πισσης (Demosthenes).

his face. Our Lord the Paparch, on the other
hand, doth not enjoy sitting in the castle like
a cat in a cherry-bay-tree, even though that
dog of a Kelt can do no more than yelp at
him. But the Christian King is totally
ignorant of this. He knoweth no more than
that he hath failed to capture Santangelo, and
that the invincible Alexander most mercifully
doth deign to give him these terms. First,
the Christian King may raise the siege, departing in peace from the inviolable City and
from Peter's Patrimony: whither, our Lord
the Paparch saith not—Gaul, Crusade, Naples,
His Sanctity specifieth not whither: but the
Christian King must go. His attempted in-
timidation of the Roman Paparch was very
blamable: but he will be permitted to retire
unmolested. Secondly, our Lord the Paparch
maketh no engagement concerning the crowns
of Naples and the rest: but the Christian
King must go. Thirdly, our Lord the Paparch
deigneth to give hostages for *vj* months to
the said Christian King, sop to uncurbable

conceit. Whom will He give, dost thou ask, as hostages in such a grave case? First, He hath given Sultán Jam; and the second's Ourself."

XI

WE *iij*, o Prospero, fetched our breath faster; and our eyes dilated, but, speaking no word, we listened.

Cesare continued, saying :

" Now these terms are not what the Keltic monkey wanted : but they are the best which he can get. Being a fool, never constant to a single idea, he hath determined to hasten southward, and to conquer Naples on his own initiative : having persuaded himself that, if he could return some day with the crowns of Naples and the rest in his hand, the Father of princes and kings would not refuse to put them on his head. So the treaty hath been signed. And, touching the matter of Sultán Jam, Our fellow-hostage, thou shalt suppose that, since the Grand Turk hath ceased to pay, he is but a burthen on our Lord the

Paparch. Also thou shalt suppose that it mattereth not a jot in whose ward he is, so long as that warden be Christian. Wherefore the magnificent Alexander most sagaciously will shift him on to the shoulders of the Christian King, whence he can be reclaimed at any time by a threat of the Dirae.[1] So much for Sultán Jam."

The speaker thrust out the protruded middle finger of his ringed right hand; and continued, saying:

" But We also are an hostage ; and, after the mass of dawn, We ride in the train of the Christian King."

My bowels began to beat like armourers' hammers. My lips retired, and left my teeth bare. I drew breath through the last, softly whistling : but as yet I knew not the true cause of mine emotions. The words which I had heard were terrible. Very great affairs were afoot: yet it did not seem that they

---

[1] Excommunication, Interdict, Deposition, and so forth.

concerned me. I was only an unnoted prince, profoundly but inexplicably agitated, with my back against an ivory door.

Gioffredo left the cardinals on the cushions, with a snort of incredulity, or despair, or disgust; and came and threw his arm around my neck, nestling against me.

But the Cardinal of Valencia continued, saying:

"Long speeches are better than short ones.[1] They give understanding, without which no action of great import can be accomplished. Dost thou admit the validity of my credentials, o Cardinal of Ferrara?"

Ippolito again offered his ear to be touched by the gigantic ring; and, standing, he asseverated:

"We are the son and servant of our Lord the Paparch, and of The Most Respectable Worship of thee speaking to Us in His name. In the words of Plato, immortal, beaming on

---

[1] τα μακρα των σμικρων λογων ἐπι προσθεν ἐστι (Eyripides).

all things, All Our money is at thy service."[1]

But now Cesare seemed to fall into a muse, yawning, playing with our impatience as the tawny tiger at our castle of Deira used to play with goats and deer.

Gioffredo left me; and went nearer, lying on the black carpet, supporting his chin on his hands, widely stretching his legs.

Ippolito sat intent, erect, on the black cushions.

I stood transfixed, staring at that queer fateful Cardinal of Valencia, who could afford to play when *iiij* hours would see him an hostage and a prisoner in an enemy's camp. Very strange it is to say, but I will tell thee, o Prospero, that, though there were *iiij* able-bodied lusty adolescents at that moment in that secret chamber, nevertheless the minds of *iij* of them were in complete abeyance; and only the mind of the fourth predominated.

---

[1] σοι δε υπαρχει μεν το εμα χρηματα (Platōn).

Wherefore we *iij* had naught to do but to listen to the mind of the Cardinal of Valencia, who at length resumed his discourse, saying:

"This ring is one of a score, which have been journeying round Christendom, on the hands of paparchal ablegates, to the Elect-Emperor Maximilian Always August, to the Catholic King[1] and Queen Don Hernando and Doña Isabella, to the Sacred King[2] Henry of the Anglicans, to the Majesties and Tranquillities and Valvasours and Supernities and Celsitudes and Magnificencies and Sublimities and Highnesses and Mightinesses and Splendours and Potencies of the Empire and Portugal and Poland and Hungary and Naples and Milan and Ferrara and Sabaudia and Genoa and Venice and Fiorenza and Mantua and Parma and Padua and Piacenza."

I am unable to tell thee, o Prospero, why

---

[1] The official style of the Kings of Spain.

[2] This would appear to be the official style of the Kings of England. It would be interesting to know when it became disused.

I refrained from roaring. But I perceived that this most feline cardinal would tell his tale in his own way and in none other. It pleased him to dally with us, watching the surging of our emotions. But anon, being satisfied, he struck with the swift talons of his stratagem, saying:

"Our Lord the Paparch is by no means at the end of His resources; and let no man think the contrary.[1] Once let Him deliver Himself from the Christian King, once let Him rid Peter's Patrimony of that pestiferous monkey, and the Holy Roman Empire, Spain, the Italian kingdoms and duchies and republics, Christendom, will league with Alexander against Gaul. In which galley We Ourself are to hold the rudder. To get the Christian King away from the City, the Sultán Jam was conducted to his camp an hour ago. When We leave this palace, We also will join the Keltic army, exposing Our life to the chances of fate." [2]

---

[1] μηδε τωι δοξηι παλιν (Aischylos).

[2] ψυχην προβαλλων ἐν κυβοισι δαιμονος (Eyripides).

Gioffredo burst in with an oath and an offer.

Cesare silenced him ; and continued, saying :

" No, Gioffredo: We will go alone. But now, o Cardinal of Ferrara, lend Us both thine ears. After the dawn-mass, We ride from the City, southward by the Appian Way toward the kingdom of Naples. So Our spies have brought news. Three hours later, We reach Velletri, beyond the frontier : where the Christian King intendeth himself to dine and sleep."

Ippolito rose, mightily towering, torvidly storming, saying :

" Hear Us now. The Most Respectable Worship of thee is the most valuable of all the Paparch's lieges. The loss of thee will be like the chopping off of Alexander's right hand. Wherefore, if it be really and truly necessary for thee to leave the City as thou sayst, let thy going be but a feint. We have here *ccc* armed barbarians to serve thee, and

K

the trained forces of Ferrara at call. We
Ourself are as strong as any man ; and, with
a mace, a mace of tempered steel, and Our
Arabian stallion between these thighs, We,
even We, will be at Velletri for Thy Worship's
rescue."

Gioffredo jumped up ; and chattered, saying :

" Let Us go in thy stead, o Valencia. Are
We not Alexander's son ? Do We not command a troop ? Is not Our wife a princess
of Aragon of Naples ? If there be question
of ransom, are We not worth as much as
thou ?"

But I still maintained phrenetic silence, keen,
alert, strenuously desiring to do something, not
knowing what to do.

Cesare waved his hand in a furry manner,
saying :

" We will not have valorously violent
rescues. None in the City may be known as
conniving at Our escape : that would insure
the Christian King's return. This is an affair

for the head, not for massive limbs. A cunning sage is here more precious than a palatine, o heraklean Ippolito. And as for thee, Gioffredo, know that there is no time in which to change Our plans. The action already is begun. The obligation is made; and cannot be evaded. But it may be annulled. If it is to be annulled, that must be done in such a way that the Christian King will not be able to prove complicity on the part of any Roman. Our Lord the Paparch must not be found out participating in conspiracy. We, His servants, must combine the columbine manner of doves with the serpentine actions of snakes. Wherefore, what is to be done must be done by others, beyond Roman territory, and (to all seeming) quite spontaneously."

It was clear that we were expected only to listen, not to advise. We were not a council: but merely pupils, in the presence of a master, who was unfolding schemes already cut and dried. We composed our bodies; and our minds attended. Cesare continued, saying:

" That blear-eyed ape of Gaul must be pinned in the kingdom of Naples as vermin is pinned in a trap. His teeth and talons must be drawn there. His army never again must return to Gaul. It must be annihilated in Italy. Wherefore, to lead the said Christian King into this trap, We Ourself will be the bait. We will go with him beyond the Roman frontier. At Velletri, We will halt with him, during the heat of the day. And, from Velletri, We will escape ; and return to the City, promptly assuming direction of the league against Gaul."

XII

Ippolito said :

"We admire the plan, but know not how an escape can be effected under such conditions."

To whom Cesare responded, saying:

"Know that the Borgia of Velletri, though little insignificant people, are of the same origin as the Roman Borgia : but they have been established in Italy many gliding lustrums longer.   Know also that the Regent of Velletri hath a son, by name Pietro Gregorio Borgia, an adolescent of parts, very anxious for a career, very friendly to Ourself, and of equal age with and similar appearance to Us.   A messenger instantly must be sent to the said Pietrogorio : who knoweth that he can make his own fortune by caring for Ours.   Wherefore, o Cardinal of Ferrara, seeing that the fame of thy collection of barbaric athletes hath come to the ears of our

Lord the Paparch, thou art commanded, by
thine obedience to the bearer of this ring thou
art commanded, to produce a swift runner here
and now."

I think that Ippolito was dazzled, at the
moment, by so distinct a recognition of his
exquisite connoisseurship of physique: for he
sat there smiling and blinking his eyes while one
might say a paternoster.

Cesare closely regarded him, until his countenance resumed its normal gravity, shewing that
the intellect within was operating; and then he
turned away, drawing Gioffredo on to his knees,
feeding him with comfits from the table.

But Ippolito approached me where I stood
rigid by the door; and would have consulted
me, naming his runners one by one, Liparo,
Hygropyrrho, Bueselvatico, Fantedifiume, Teres,
Lo Skytho, Lo Skoto, the sleek one, the
supple redhead, the wild bull, the servant of
the sea, the smooth-fleshed one, the Skythian,
the Skot, demanding my judgment of each.

But I could not think of anything saving the

great good fortune of Pietrogorio, my stars
being malignant. I envied and hated him as
much as possible; and I wished to occupy his
place. There came before mine eyes a phantasm of my maid, as she stood before me at
Vatican, with her dear brows so finely lifted
and her sweet lips so rapturously trembling,
pitying me and urging me. Yet, here I was,
stone-still, unable to move, for I knew neither
whither nor how.

Ippolito looked at me with inquiry. I
vacantly returned his gaze. And anon, having
led me aside, he opened the door.

The wedge of Numidians, basaltine, gigantic,
turned to face him, making a path for him. A
vermilion page advanced, impertinently bending to the ground. That one had the form of
a young Hyakinthos, and the face of a beautiful
white fiend framed in a web of buttercup-
coloured hair. Ippolito commanded him to
summon the chief chamberlain.

The page's parthenean voice shrilled through
the outer antechambers.

The chief chamberlain trotted toward us, bustling and genuflecting. To whom Ippolito delivered a mandate, saying:

"Lo Skoto, in secret."

The chief chamberlain fled. In flying, he swept before him all the pages and gentlemen until the door of the private stairs was passed, driving them out of sight and hearing, leaving only those mute eunuchs of the Numidian guard. Anon, he returned accompanied by a half-savage runner, a lanky, stone-deaf youth of the age of *xviiij* years bought out of the horrible and ultimate Britains. This animal was pushed into the secret chamber; and the door again was shut.

I shall describe this singular barbarian, o Prospero, who was of astonishing leanness, stepping like a prancing horse, and very archaic as to his aspect. He was clad in an oblong cloth, chequered in brown and green and yellow. The lower quarter of the said cloth was belted in folds round his waist. The upper three-quarters were folded together lengthways, and

passed upward, behind his back, over his left
shoulder and breast; and the end was tucked
into the front of the right side of his belt.[1]   A
goat-skin pouch[2] depended from the fore-part
of the said belt.   All the rest of him was uncovered.   His arms were very long and very
thin.   His breast was enormous.   His long
legs also were very lean, but round and sinewy.
His feet were horny.   His heavy head was
pear-shaped: the brow, white: the cheeks and
nose and pointed jaw, thickly freckled: the hair,
a nasty light mud-coloured brown knot on the
crown; and the steel-coloured eyes awkwardly
wavered behind small slits, unlashed, sly.   His
stench was abominable.

The Cardinal of Valencia sniffed at the
perfumed amber ball which was chained to
his left wrist; and, having examined Lo Skoto's
points in the way which one useth for horses,
he appeared to be satisfied.   So he came to us

---

[1] This " oblong cloth " seems to be the original
" kilt and plaid " in one garment.

[2] Obviously a fifteenth century " sporran."

sitting on the cushions; and demanded of Ippolito that a mage should be summoned, who could cause the runner to sleep instantly and heavily during a half-hour without impeding his speed thereafter.

Ippolito went into the antechamber, commanding the service of Messer Nerone Diotisalvi, the mage who tolerated natural death by strangling after the conclave which elected the Piccolhuomini.[1] But, to occupy the time which preceded the arrival of this one, Cesare took writing materials; and wrote this letter:

"*To Our well-beloved Don Pietro Gregorio Borgia of Velletri.*

"*These with speed, speed, speed.*[2]

"*Our Lord the Paparch suddenly sendeth Us as hostage with the Christian King, leaving*

---

[1] Alexander the Sixth's successor, Pius the Third (Francesco de' Piccolhuomini). What particular cantrips Diotisalvi engaged in at that conclave, the gods only know. Anyhow, he richly deserved a hanging long before he got it.

[2] "Cito: Cito: Cito:" in the original holograph.

Us no opportunity of attending to Our proper affairs. Wherefore thou art to know that the bearer of these letters is an unruly slave, who (if We remained here) should tolerate not more than one hour of Our private pillory, distended as to arms and legs, not stringently enough to harm, but stringently enough, with divers apt and commodious actions on the flesh of his bare back. For which cause, o well-beloved Pietro-gorio, by the affection which thou dost nourish for Us, thy trusty kinsman, We lay it upon thee to treat our said slave conveniently as aforesaid, with all other order known to thy piety, that he may have amended his said naughty ways before Our return. And so earn Our gratitude.

"C. CAR^{al} DE VALENCIA."

When we were permitted to peruse the screed, Gioffredo denounced it as nonsense. Ippolito uttered the opinion that it meant what it did not say. But I, being perplexed and angry, gave favour to my tongue.

Cesare, having guffawed at our stolidity, said:
"Be it known unto these princes that Our
use is to keep, in every city, at least one
adolescent on whom We may depend in need.
Such an one in Velletri is Pietrogorio, prepared
for any emergency, prompt to serve; and he
will know what ought to be done. Furthermore, if the Kelts, or Colonna, or Orsini, or
Savelli, or Dellarovere, or Cajetani, or any other
bandits, shall catch the runner of such a message as this, having read it, will they not rather
most hilariously hasten him on to his whipping?"

We *iij* laughed, conceding the point.

Messer Nerone presently entered, indulging
himself in a phrenetic spasm of obeisances,
chirruping like a slow tomtit. He was antique,
humpty-backed. He spoke always in mono-
tone, using a high shrill scream with most
exasperating deliberation.

At whom Ippolito rushed, explaining what
was to be done. We others stuffed our kerchieves in our nostrils, standing laughing near
Lo Skoto, anxious to see the doing.

But the physician forthwith crossed the room to the table where the wine was and the water, prattling of the virtues of belladonna and stramonium. There, standing with his back to Lo Skoto and having taken *ij* little silver pots from his burse, he put a pinch from each into a cup of wine. This cup he put on a salver with another similar cup which he filled with pure water ; and so he brought them both to the runner.

As this was being done, the *ij* cardinals and Gioffredo held a parley on the cushions : but I moved toward the window, whence I watched all, unseen, breathing cleaner air.

Messer Nerone offered the water to the runner. Lo Skoto reluctantly sipped it, longingly leering at the wine. The mage, having pretended to assure himself that no one was observing, simulated a sudden access of liberality ; and offered the wine instead. It was done most admirably, with absolute art.

Lo Skoto gulched down the infected potion, stroking himself, vacuously grinning.

The mage replaced the salver with the cups on the ivory table. The Cardinal of Valencia took the *ij* little silver pots from him, and pouched them: giving him the jewel with its slight chains from the back of his own hand, and putting him outside the ivory door in the antechamber among the Numidians with a word of dismissal.

As he went, I touched his hump for luck; for it seemed that I needed all the aids which fortune had in store, my stars being most malignant. We heard the shrill whining of his voice dying away as he was escorted beyond the antechambers.

The door having been shut, we continued to entertain ourselves, paying no attention to the drugged runner, except with the corners of our eyes.

But I was staring at the innumerable lights of the waxen torches, reflected in endless vistas in the polished ivory of the circular walls and the dome of the roof, until mine eyes were dazzled by the sheen. And I chafed: being in that agony of bewilderment when the whole world seems to whirl round, near, very near, but just out of reach. For nothing is more exasperating than to find oneself still and alone, when everything else is in myriads violently moving, eluding one's grasp.

Anon, the runner suddenly started as though a phantom had touched him unawares. He cast suspicious glances round him : but we *iiij* were in the middle of the chamber, while he was alone by the door. We stood up, openly looking at him as though we were astounded at his audacity: for, in starting, he had knocked down the double-cross, golden, which leaned against the pedestal of the ivory faun near him, nor did he attempt to replace it. Indeed, his eyes began to glare like those of one who unadvisedly had looked upon a cluster of hobgoblins. His knees also began to bend like those of one pressed downward by an incubus, gently, irresistibly. Anon he became prone on the black carpet.

Having approached him, Cesare opened one

of his eyes with thumb and index-finger. Naught but white was seen. Having pinched together *iij* barleycorns' length of the freckled flesh of the neck, the said cardinal transfixed the same with a needle-point from Ippolito's hand-case. But the sleeper soundly slept.

Cesare returned to the black cushions ; and seated himself by side of Ippolito, saying :

" Let Us have the skin of this barbarian's back."

Gioffredo assisted me. We left the runner in possession of nothing but himself. He was very heavy and inert ; and we pulled him about rather roughly. Anon, having dragged him to the feet of the cardinals, we laid him out on the black carpet, limp as a freshly-made cadaver, a lean long form, huge of loin, the breast deeply arched, puny and narrow of shoulder and arm. The tan of the sinuous legs faded at the middle of the thighs : thence, to the ribs on the right side and to the shoulder on the left side, there was dazzling whiteness. Having inspected him, we turned him downward ; and left him, eagerly fixing our gaze on the Cardinal of Valencia.

That purpled person produced from his burse a tiny crystal vial containing a flesh-coloured liquid, viscous and opaque as cream, with a little brush of very fine hogs bristles. Having unstopped the vial, he gave it into Ippolito's ready hand ; and dipped the brush. We became conscious of a certain fœtor, mysterious, mephitic.

Cesare said :

" Know that ye are savouring a solution in spirit of the juice of an Indian fig,[1] which We took from Messer Leone Abrabanel of Naples. Know also that We habitually bereave mages of their drugs when We have seen the method of using and the effect of the same : for a prince very often hath need of such matters."

Mark well, o Prospero, those words of wisdom.

Thus he spoke : but we signified assent with

---

[1] I am inclined to think that this is what we call indiarubber.

L

our eyebrows very intently watching his actions. He began to write with the brush upon the runner's back.

But a terrific catastrophe instantly happened.

For, at the first touch of the said brush on the top of the left shoulder-blade, the malignance of his stars caused the sleeper to think fit to move his head, and to attempt to rise. Immense confusion instantly invaded the secret chamber.

Cesare sprang up, vociferating maledictions. Ippolito stopped the vial ; and pouched it, preparing himself to rebut accusations of treachery. Gioffredo danced up and down like a cat who inopportunely hath stepped on an oven.

Lo Skoto with a bound was on his feet, phrenetic with fear, capering hither and thither, babbling in an unknown savage jargon. Upon whom I launched myself like a flash of white thunder.

But, before I could touch and crush his flesh with mine, Cesare whipped a raging poignard into him, and out : a clever Roman thrust upward through the heart from the stomach. The runner wriggled and choked, spouting red blood ; and fell. He kicked the carpet *iiij* times very quickly ; and writhed ; and died straight. I never have seen so short an agony.

The Cardinal of Valencia at once recovered his equanimity ; and dried his poignard in the knot of dead hair, saying to Ippolito :

"Pardon, o Cardinal of Ferrara, on account of this puddle on thy carpet. It is not caused by malice but by necessity. But now, before we consider new plans, let us be rid of this carrion, secretly."

Ippolito continued to gaze at the carcase.

But, by favour of some benignant star, my wits seemed to be coming back to me. I began to know, one by one in order, the things which I ought to do.

Wherefore, I beckoned to Gioffredo to take the ankles : but I myself took the hollow arm-pits; and terribly the head waggled between. In this manner we flung the dead slave from the balcony : but, after we had heard the splash of his fall in Tiber, we returned, expecting new events.

Still was the gaze of Ippolito fixed on the mess on the carpet. Cesare walked like a tiger to and fro in a fume. Now my vision was clear ; my stars being very benignant : nor did perplexity blind me any more to my chance.

XIII

HAVING collected the vesture of the runner, I placed myself in the way of the Cardinal of Valencia, whom I addressed, saying :

" Tiber beareth that dead barbarian to the sea ; and I, o Lord Cardinal, will be Thy Most Respectable Worship's angel." [1]

With which words I flung down my night-gown of ermine.

Cesare instantly stopped, inquiring whether I could run. To whom my mouth gave no response : for my form and membrature testified the thing. His glances impinged upon me, bringing the hot blood from mine heart ; and looking down, I saw my breast reddening as though stricken with the flat of the hand.

Ippolito suddenly interrupted, saying :

" Can he run indeed ? But he can run, an

---

[1] " ἄγγελος " (messenger) in the original holograph.

he will, with the superhuman swiftness and endurance of Wing - footed Hermes, or of Asahel who ran like a wild roe in the Sacred Scriptures."

Thus was Cesare satisfied. He said :

" Be then Our angel, o white prince ; and run for Us and for thyself."

In this manner I became the first of the *iiij* adolescents there present.

At my commandment, pages brought certain matters from the wardrobe, depositing them at my feet : and, retiring, left us alone to make preparations for the running.

I belted the runner's cloth on my loins, letting the larger portion hang down behind, so that my back was bare. Ippolito very carefully folded *ij* squares of tanned buckskin round my feet ; and firmly bandaged them with thongs of the same. Thus garbed, I turned my face to the ivory door, exposing the flesh of my back as the Cardinal of Valencia willed.

Thereon he began to write cyphers with the brush. The viscous liquid, which he used seemed somewhat to sting and bite me : but I clenched my teeth and fists, and remained immovable; and anon the little pangs evanesced. He covered my back with writing from shoulder to shoulder and below to my middle, *vij* lines in all.   While he was writing, he explained the thing, saying :

"These characters, which now are wet and glossy, will become invisible when they are dried, being of the same colour as the substance on which We write.   Such is the nature of this magic, that neither sweat nor water will affect it.   Ye have seen the letters, which We wrote in ink upon the paper, to be naught but a mere blind.   The prince will carry those letters in the goatskin pouch ; and anyone may read them.   But he beareth the real message on his proper body ; and no Roman ever hath seen that message : for ye see that each letter evanisheth as We write it.   Nor hath this angel himself seen it : for no adolescent can see his own back.   But Pietrogorio alone will see it: for he will rub this fine white flesh with soot which, adhering to the cyphers, will render them visible when the back which beareth them shall have been cleansed with washing."

Thus he spoke : but I was thinking of my reward, though a reward was not named : for I knew that great rewards would be due for such a service ; and furthermore the cardinal had said that I was about to run for myself as well as for him. Moreover I knew from his way of handling me, very gentle, very urbane, what all the world knoweth now, *videlicet*, that, from the moment when he first saw how my stars had made me, the splendid Cardinal of Valencia loved and honoured me.

And, when the matter was completed, I demanded a poignard for mine equipment, lest the said Pietrogorio, or any other person instigated by the devil, being strange to me, should try to fulfil the mandate of the letters which I carried in the goatskin pouch : for it was not meet that a prince of my quality, nameless, nearly naked, and without credentials as I was, should submit to pillory and stripes.

And so, having folded the upper part of the cloth together lengthways, I passed it under my right arm and across my breast and over my left shoulder, fixing the end in the belt, so that the wind of my swift movement should not cause it to impede me. And, having composed mine hair as tightly as possible in my nightcap, I at length was ready to run.

Sumpter-mules, which bore the cardinal's valises, were waiting in the first court. Gioffredo donned one of my riding-habits of white doeskin, while a litter was being prepared for me. Covered with a cloak, I was placed therein. Two decurions attended us, chosen for secrecy and fidelity. We crossed Tiber by the Island, riding very quietly by Saints Nereys and Achilleys to the Gate of Saint Sebastian.

During the journey in the silent litter, I was able to recollect myself. It was more than ever plain to me that I was the chief prince in this adventure. Wherefore I did not hesitate at taking the government into mine own

hands, even to the issuing of commandments to the cardinals and to the Prince of
Squillace.

On mine emergence, bare-limbed, light-
hearted, I assured Cesare that his errand
was as good as done ; and dismissed him
with Ippolito to the Keltic camp. They
swore : but they smiled at me ; and they
went.

But I bade Gioffredo to return to the Estense
Palace, there to rest in my bed, in order that
he might be able to render the assistance
which I would need in the morning after
my running. For I was intending myself
to return, a-horseback if possible, by the
upper road,[1] that I might not encounter the
Kelts swarming along the lower. Wherefore I bade him to bring his troop and
my litter to the Lateran Gate at the first

---

[1] The New Appian Way which diverged from the
Old Appian Way, avoiding the fortified tomb of
Cecilia Metella, generally a nest of brigands in the pay
of bandit barons.

hour of the day,[1] there to attend about a league outside the gate until my coming.

He agreed ; and, embracing me, gave me good luck in my going. Nothing delayed me longer, and I took to the road.

---

[1] 6 a.m.

XIIII

THE night was very dark and cold. A little horned moon gave as much light as let me see the riband of road stretched out before me, and no more. The lines of ruined tombs on both sides were only shapeless blacknesses silhouetted on blacker blackness. I cared nothing then for the pleasures of sight.

The cool fresh breath of Lady Night greeted my nostrils, and caressed my flesh as I ran.

The hum of the City very soon was left behind. I heard naught save the sighs of the sleeping earth and the quick delicate patter of my well-shod footsteps.

The aromatic flavour of herbs growing by the roadside was on my lips: from time to time my protruded tongue tasted the cool sweetness.

All my body tingled with the pleasure of swift movement.

I thought of nothing at all : letting my forces collect and develop only in pressing onward with long light striding. I knew that the triumph of our Lord the Paparch depended on me, that I was alone and unprotected : but I felt myself to be so terribly strong that I could have shouted for very gladness. I saved my breath ; and continued running. More than this I cannot tell thee of my running, o mine own mercurial Prospero : for I myself know nothing more.

I went with extreme caution by Cajetani's Tower :[1] but the darkness of midnight and the malignance of that baron's stars favoured me, so that the watch did not perceive my passing. That was the only real piece of danger in mine enterprize. Having escaped it, I stretched myself to the fulness of my speed.

Anon the straight white way lost itself

---

[1] The tomb of Cecilia Metella, apparently then used as a fortress by the bandit baron Cajetani.

beneath a carpet of grass.[1] I guided my course between the gaunt ruins of the tombs on each hand. I could not pass Solfatara[2] without refreshing myself; and, having denuded my body reeking with sweat, I plunged into the pool again and again until all my flesh was benumbed. I will tell thee, o Prospero, that thy father at that moment was in a mood for violent feats. My strength was multiplied a thousand times by the cold water : but the heart in my breast rejoiced greatly, because I knew that I was in a way to break my fetters. Wherefore I set out again at augmented speed, desiring to accomplish mine errand, but also to leave behind me the disgusting stench of the pool.

Hereafter, in my running, I thought of my maid in the City, who knew not what great deeds her loving lover was doing in order that

---

[1] The Old Appian Way was disused between Palombaro and Bovillae. Near the latter place the juncture with the New Appian Way occurs.

[2] An antique sulphur spring.

he might win her. But these thoughts went near to impede my progress : for which cause I postponed them until a more opportune occasion.

The night became more obscure ; and I ran for a very long time keeping my mind in abeyance, concentrating all my physical force on my running.

Anon the moon set ; and there was no light but dim starlight. It behoved me to go very cautelously : for, at Albano was Savelli, fortified, rebellious. Wherefore, having prayed to my proper divinities as well as to those who were the protectors of my maid, beseeching them that they would bring me to the herborough where I would be, I ascended the hill, passing that city on the right ; and made my way by the lake into Aricia.

I was running by faith and not by sight. The road was much more difficult by cause of the many ups and downs. But I did not slacken speed: for I knew that my stars were as benignant as possible.

Cinthyanum[1] was still asleep as I fled through its street, silent, vacant. In all my journey indeed I encountered no one of human origin, clearly shewing that the gods approved my course. I might have rested safely anywhere in the dark. But I would not : for I feared lest my limbs should stiffen ; and there was in my mind only the sole desire of fulfilling my mission. Wherefore I continued to run faster and faster, knowing how very grateful is rest after activity very strenuous, very prolonged.

Anon the darkness of the night gave way to a certain timid greyness, whereby I was enabled to follow the windings of the road with less caution. But by cause that dawn was near, I put forth all my vigour. I was conscious only that my legs were swinging to and fro with no effort, lightly-flying, space-devouring. I was happy, by cause of them, by cause that my flesh glowed in the cold air, by cause that I was alive and doing.

---

[1] Genzano di Roma.

Naught else gave me happiness, here, at the end of my journey. So I entered Velletri, through the gate, with the dawn.

M

XV

My shouts for the palace of the Regent, and the fierceness of my mien, brought me instantly to Pietrogorio.

Had I not known that the Cardinal of Valencia had remained in the City, and that none had passed me on the road, I should have suspected magic of the particular kind called bilocation, by means of which the golden-thighed Pythagoras was seen and heard to lecture, at the same day and hour, in the two widely distant cities of Metapontion and Tayromenion : for the aspect of this adolescent was precisely similar to that of the other who had sent me. But my stars told me that they must be two and not one : for which cause I did not hesitate to present the written letters from the goatskin pouch.

Pietrogorio permitted himself to laugh while

he was reading : in which diversion I did not omit to join, although, fearing lest he might stray unduly into error, I kept my poignard handy. Anon I took the first opportunity of acquainting him with the quality of mine estate ; and he instantly withdrew me from the court, where he had been about to exercise some horses, conducting me to a secret apartment allotted to him by the Regent, his father.

He said :

"If, as We believe, the truth is being told, it will be known unto this prince what other matters must be done before the whole message can come to Our knowledge."

To whom I instantly responded, saying :

"Let a shovelful of soot be brought, and several bucketfuls of water for washing ; and anon this noble will not be prevented from completing the said message for himself."

The things having been brought into an empty part of the stables, near by the boxes where the horses were, but separate therefrom by a wooden wall, I divested myself of the long cloth ; and stood still, keeping my poignard in my hands, alert to unsheathe it.

Pietrogorio understood ; and he also knew that I understood. So far we had gone step by step in turn ; and now he was to advance to the last stage.

Taking the soot in handfuls, he rubbed the flesh of my back therewith. I felt it dropping, with odious softness, on my loins and on the calves of my legs: for I was standing very stiffly. Sometimes, looking over my shoulders, I saw that the shining whiteness of me was becoming as dully black as a Moor: but, having so degraded myself as to run across Campagna in a barbaric slave's garb, I placed no demurrer against this last abomination. But I promised myself many very long ablutions, elaborate, exquisite, in the moment after my return to the City. Indeed, I was not in a condition to place remonstrances of any kind at that time : for, whether my message pleased him or irked him, I was at

Pietrogorio's mercy for present accommodation and refreshment as well as for means of return. So I submitted in silence.

Having blacked half of me thoroughly, making me a piebald prince for the first and last time, he fetched a horse-block near me; and, standing thereon, he poured *iiij* bucketfuls of water over me.

It greatly refreshed me : but I grieved when I saw that the water, in flowing over my back, carried away the superfluous soot, trickling over every part of me save my breast and mine arms which I held upward. The first bucketful ran off in inky streams : the second and third were greyer and still greyer ; and the fourth was almost clear. But the flesh of me remained of a terrible dirtiness ; and I stood still, sodden, unclean, beginning to shiver, very strenuously expecting an end.

Pietrogorio dismounted from the horse-block ; and inspected the visible cyphers on my back. Incontinent he uttered the greatest shout which I ever have heard from the throat of one adolescent. It was so full of surprize, of delight, of urgency, that I turned upon him, eagerly inquiring.

But emotion transfixed him for the moment. The intense expression of his countenance taught me that he was collecting his energies for some tremendous effort, that he was in the throes of labour with some huge idea.

Anon, his plan was born; and the tension was relaxed. Not forgetful of good manners, even at such a moment, he thus addressed me:

" Order shall be given for the comfort and the entertainment due to Thy Most Illustrious Potency. But We Ourself beg to be excused from attendance, seeing that We have in hand the vital welfare of Our patron, on whose account We are willing to die : for it seemeth to Us that another messenger must go to Cinthyanum on the instant."

To whom I promptly responded, saying :

" Give Us the means of riding, and We

Ourself will be that messenger : for We desire
nothing better than to emulate Thy Nobility
in serving the Cardinal of Valencia to the
uttermost; and it is clear that We shall serve
Ourself at the same time, seeing that Cinthyanum lieth on the high road to the City."

Thus I spoke, letting the fire of mine eyes
add force to the words ; and Pietrogorio saw
that the thing must be so.   He himself is, as
thou knowest, o Prospero, more a man of
deeds than of words ; and, thereafter, we
spoke little but did much in a few moments of
time.

While I girded on the runner's garb again,
he saddled an horse for me, shouting meanwhile for his people to bring the juice of a
live goose pressed to death for me to drink,
and to rub my stiffening legs with mugwort in
oil.   Which was done.

Anon I leaped into the saddle; and he led
me through the gateway alone.   There, he
gave me the little gold ring with the carbuncle
(which thy mother, o Prospero, weareth on her

neck-chain), signing for the use of mine ear. Having bent to him, he whispered:

" Present this ring to the postmaster of Cinthyanum, as a sign that all the horses in that city are bought up by the Cardinal of Valencia."

Thus having spoken, he sent me flying away at a gallop, mightily striking the stallion on the rump with his fist.

XVI

I HAD no more than a superficial knowledge of what was doing now. But I was returning to the City; and that sufficed for my satisfaction. Little vulgar boys gibed at my disgraceful aspect as I rode through the streets. At another time I would have cut out their tongues: but, then, I did not even stop to frown at them. Little simpering girls, going to mass with the nuns of their convent, pretended to shudder at the dirty, detestable, but not unshapely legs so shamelessly exposed: but I did not even kiss my fingers. Every moment now brought me nearer to my proper maid. I thought of nothing else as I flew along the road: but I grieved a little by cause that I had no spurs, and the whip (which I had snatched up at parting) was but a slight one. Moreover, I had left my poignard in the stable.

But, when I drummed with mine heels on my beast's barrel, the sodden leather of my footgear emitted certain squelching noises, amusing to the rider, terrific to the ridden: for he augmented his speed in a very agreeable manner, not needing any other incitement.

So I came to Cinthyanum; and, having done my business with the postmaster, I pursued my course without drawing rein.

When I reached the summit of the hill by the ruins,[1] I saw (in the ravine before me) an approaching troop. Mine eyes were so blinded by my sweat and the dust of my furious riding, that (though I perceived the glint of the sun on loricate mail-coats and on cross-bows) I could not see clearly whether these were worn and borne by friends or foes.

But I knew that it was easier to ride

---

[1] I don't quite know what these ruins are, unless they are the remnants of the Villa of Vitellius on Monte Gentile : but, if this be the case, Don Tarquinio was off the main road. There are plenty of ravines between Genzano and Aricia, now spanned by the viaducts of Pius the Ninth.

through a squadron from an high place, than for an ascending squadron to obstruct precipitate attack. Wherefore I goaded mine horse to extra speed with terrific shoutings as well as with the thuds of mine heels; and it seemed that I was going very quickly.

But the beast, having run away four times for his own pleasure and being now constrained to run for mine, was becoming exhausted; and I myself was becoming sore and rather feeble from the stress of my night's adventure: moreover, I was famishing with hunger. For which causes we came down the steep hill with less impetus than I had designed; and nothing would have been done at the bottom in the way of smashing a passage through the advancing troop.

The said troop, indeed, did not wait for the onslaught: but, to my immense surprise, ranged itself by the sides of the road laughing very loudly indeed.

But I, indignant at gratuitous contumely, erected myself on my saddle, straight and filthy (for I had come down the hill lying along the horse's back the better to avoid wounds during the proposed swift passage); and I indignantly looked about for one of mine own estate whom I might call to account. And, while I was looking, my beast rocked and fell dead: but I made shift to leap clear of him, in order to meet mine own torture and death in a princely manner.

But I had fallen into no worse hands than those of the chubby Gioffredo. That one instantly began to chatter: to whose inquiries I would not respond, until he had dismounted one of his own kataphractors[1] in order to give me a new horse; and then I insisted that we should hasten toward the City.

So we galloped together like Kastor and Polydeykes: but the dismounted kataphractor rode a-pillion with one of his comrades. And, as we went, I gave a little news of my deeds to

---

[1] Mail-clad cavalry with cross-bows. Pietrogorio's tombstone at Velletri names him as the lieutenant of Caesar Borgia's kataphractors.

Gioffredo until my breath failed me. The remnant I kept for the business of riding as quickly as possible; for I was very anxious to make an end.

When I lapsed into silence, Gioffredo began to be garrulous. What he said was not important. He had spent an hour of the night with his wife at Traspontina. But it pleased me to hear that impatience and a kind heart had constrained him to leave long before the time, and had sent him so great a distance along the road to mine assistance. And I eagerly desired to reach the Lateran Gate: for there (so he said) the litter was waiting, wherein I longed to seclude myself, by cause of the sordid condition of my body, which shame forbade me to exhibit in the City, and by cause that fatigue was affecting me very gravely indeed.

Anon we reached the place; and, having been lifted on to the soft cushions, the curtains were drawn about me. Instantly I fell asleep: for which cause, o Prospero, I am unable to write the history of my progress from the Lateran Gate to the Estense Palace. But there I awoke, as the mules halted with a jerk in the first court.

I peeped between the curtains ; and I saw the double-cross and the torches of the cardinal's estate disappearing up the steps of the audience-chamber : from which portent I augured that it would be useless to try to approach Ippolito until such time when he should have finished the morn's business of dispensing justice to his family.

But, that I might come at him as soon as possible, I advised Gioffredo to dismiss the decurions, and himself to accompany me as I was, mixing unnoted with the motley of clients, parasites, flatterers, men-at-arms, chamberlains, pages, chaplains, athletes, poets, painters, merchants, officials, secretaries, servitors, women, who were thronging into the audience-chamber.

So we did. But, though we were able to enter, we could not penetrate to the front of the crowd, having come in behind all the others. I myself was too drowsy and too stiff to care whether I spoke then or at another time. My only idea was to refrain from interrupting the natural order of events, and to wait for an opportunity: for I saw that my stars had become malignant. Wherefore I restrained Gioffredo from certain violent demonstrations which he was preparing ; and together we found a corner quieter than the others.

Here, by the marble wall, we sat on the settle of marble, out of the stink and confusion of the mob at the front.

XVII

In order to prevent myself from falling again into slumber, I carefully noted the white walls and the cornice of shields, spade-shaped, richly blazoned, and the Byzantine tapestries which depended therefrom. Nor did the grandeur of Ippolito on his vermilion throne, listening to the chaplains who intoned the Office of None, escape my notice. In the same manner I assiduously attended when the day's business was begun. At first it was uninteresting.

While the auditors whispered advice in the cardinal's ears, and while the secretaries recorded events in huge tomes or wrote at his dictation, I put myself to count the gilded coffers of the oaken roof. This casting upward of mine eyes made me more drowsy than ever: but I knew that, if once I permitted myself to sleep, my sleep would be a stupor from which even an earthquake would not awaken me. Wherefore I constrained myself to note all that was going on : lest I should lose a chance of declaring mine achievement. For it must be clear to thee, o Prospero, that, when I ran as the Cardinal of Valencia's angel, I ran as the Cardinal of Ferrara's familiar, to which last it behoved me to render an account as soon as possible, as well for relieving him from his obligation to the credentials sent by our Lord the Paparch as for mine own deliverance, first, from the filth of my body, secondly, from the rigour which was paralyzing my limbs, thirdly, from the Great Ban which so direly was afflicting me. For I did not doubt but that the last would be the reward of my running.

To pass the time, I entertained myself with thoughts of my maid, as soon as I had convinced Gioffredo of my determination to remain silent. He, being more than a little fatigued, took a nap, after cursing me for a sulky prince. I

N

promised myself an abundance of felicity in the contemplation of Hersilia, when she should have heard of my *viiij* leagues' journey through the lonely night: for it is very pleasant to be pitied and admired by one's lover when one has striven strenuously and successfully. I tried to be deaf to the hubbub in front of me, while I indulged my mind as aforesaid: but it was merely another insidious way to sleep. Wherefore, having rejected it, I dismissed my proper affairs, and alertly attended to the others. They were as follows.

The master of pages exhibited, to the cardinal, the monthly sheaf of the boys' specimens of handwriting. Ippolito having inspected the same, dictated to a secretary to be written neatly on a bad one: " Gianlucido, write thus or better here and now."

The master of pages retired, to see it done: but Ippolito signed some billets authorizing sundry expenditures for household stuff. The notary executed them ; and the datary sealed them.

The steward brought a plebeian page, who had been caught in the act of spitting idly into the rainwater tank of the cardinal's bathing-chamber. The rascal was condemned to be stripped in the courtyard, and to be spat upon by *x* of his companions during half-an-hour. Order was issued for covering the said tank with stout canvas.

The mistress of the women shrilly complained that one Fulgencia, a laundry-maid, was refusing to be married by the barber's son, to whom she had been betrothed one year. Interrogated whether she could shew cause for so culpable a defection, the said Fulgencia responded, saying: No. And sucked her thumb. The mistress of the women was impowered to whip her, in the presence of *iij* maids, every Friday at the ninth hour of the day, until the marriage should have been consummate. The said Fulgencia, having bellowed for instant nuptials, was conveyed to the chapel with the said barber's son, *iiij* witnesses, and one chaplain, to be married forthwith.

The oil-merchant appealed against the steward, who was intending to cause him to bear the loss of a consignment of his merchandize which had been stolen, on the Ostian Way, by brigands in the pay of the bandit Cardinal Giuliano Dellarovere desirous of building a new cathedral.[1] The said appeal was admitted.

The vegetable-merchant very brazenly came forward, producing a similar appeal. But the steward confronted him with proofs of his fraud. His appeal was rejected, and his privilege was cancelled ; and the steward had commandment to purchase vegetables in future from the deceiver's rival.

The slave-merchant offered for sale *ij* young Indian acrobats, saying that Cardinal Rafaele Riarj wished to have them. They performed divers tricks of agility, which Ippolito ap-

---

[1] He did build it two years later (A.D. 1497). This example of the fifteenth century method of raising cathedral-building-funds may be compared with that of the twentieth.

plauded; and he gave order that, on the physician certifying them to be healthy and their bodies without blemish, the treasurer should pay the price. They were extremely slim of figure; and their flesh was as yellow as dew-kissed pumpkins gleaming in the sunlight.

The chief equerry had order to water the horses daily in Tiber, beyond the Portuensian Gate, seeing that the Keltic army was gone away.

Order was issued for the burial of *ij* mercenaries, who had been found murdered outside the barbacan at dawn, having gone out at night without their mail-shirts. Order was issued for *ij* masses to be intoned for their souls' repose.

Order was issued for *iij* masses to be intoned for the repose of the soul of one without a name, who had died improvisedly and suddenly.

The absurd Messer Nerone Diotisalvi was required on pain of the minor torments to apply himself more assiduously to his studies in the magic arts. For it will be clear to thee, o Prospero, that, had it not been for that mage's ignorance of his proper craft, homicide would not have been necessary.

Permission was granted to the firelighter to become served by *ij* extra boys, if the weather should continue to be cold.

The new goldsmith offered a crucifix for purchase. Ippolito, having inspected the piece, gave order that the wretch should be buffeted by all and singular, from the audience-chamber to the gate of the barbacan, by cause that he contumeliously had used carelessness in making the Image of the Divine Heros.

A strange poet, in a dark-green wig resembling sea-weeds, declaimed a sonnet in praise of a bee's nipples ; and he was derided.

A very young painter, shy, rather rosy-faced, exhibited a panel whereon he had depicted the Divine Herakles and the gruesome Hydra. To whom the treasurer had order to pay *xx* gold sequins.

Ippolito complained that the tallow-scraper had neglected to scrape tallow from *iiij* stairs, whereby the attire of a certain chamberlain (whose name I have forgotten) had been rendered indecorous, and the cardinalitial shins themselves liable to divers incommodious abrasions. The said misdemeanant was produced ; and charged with his crime. He blubbered. Order was issued that he should tolerate *vij* stripes in honour of the Apostles. He yelled.

The master of the pages exhibited the amended specimen of handwriting. Ippolito, having denominated it still very evil, dictated to a secretary to be written very neatly thereupon : "Gianlucido, write thus or better before to - morrow, or bid farewell to thine hide."

The captain of the mercenaries accused a Turkish arbalister of having murdered a baptized Dacian slinger treacherously, in a brawl, at the sixth hour of the night : also, of having torn out the said Dacian's heart, eating the same, hot, in contempt of our most holy faith. Order was issued that the said Turk, having been conveniently tormented, should tolerate natural death by strangulation within the hour : that his carcase should hang in the place of exposition till avemmaria, and then be thrown into Tiber at a mile below the Portuensian Gate.

Two tormentors introduced the miscreant tallow-scraper before the dais, loudly bawling. He was a sturdy Trasteverino of about the age of *xiij* years, dark-coloured and big-eyed, and tough and sinewy as a young wolf. Having placed him, they tied his wrists behind him with the end of a coil of rope, deftly tossing the other end over a beam in the roof, and pulling it taut ; and so they waited.

Ippolito was smelling to an orange infected with rose-attar : for indeed the fœtor of the mob in the audience-chamber was most putid. He threw the fruit to a favourite page ; and I augured from the expression on his physiognomy that he was about to manifest abnormal sagacity. He pretended that he understood not the business which was afoot ; and demanded the reason for these preparations.

The tallow-scraper ceased his clamour, concentrating his gaze on the cardinal.

The first tormentor responded, saying :

"The Most Illustrious Purpled Person will choose to hear the rogue's confession of his crime."

Ippolito said :

"We have heard."

The first tormentor volubly expostulated, saying :

"But not under The Question, o Most Illustrious : for none can believe a creature who is neither clerk nor noble, unless he (first) shall have been hauled upward by the drawn-back wrists and (secondly) shall have been dropped suddenly to within a span from the floor. It is the torture of hanging from dislocated shoulders which alone insureth a true confession."

Thus having spoken, he instantly pulled the rope; and the boy ascended high over the heads of all.

But that rascal, being very sinewy and very

quick-witted, did not wait for the dislocation of his shoulders. For, drawing up his legs and clenching his teeth as he left the floor, he instantly pressed his bound hands downward on his buttocks, with admirable force, twisting round and round like an athlete.

Applause began to be heard. The boy's throat curved stiffly backward; and his breasts and shoulders resembled tan-coloured knots as he hung up there. He bended his legs further and further back; and, by degrees, he contrived to grasp his own ankles, relaxing the strain on his sinews, and hanging face-downward in a delicate semicircle like a strung bow hanging by its string.

But Ippolito went on speaking to the tormentor, saying very quickly:

"What thou hast said is purely silly. Our chamberlain's split hosen, and the tallow on Our stairs, proclaim the crime. The boy's office is to look that Our floors lack tallow. No confession is needed, with The Question or without. Let him come down. Give him his whipping.

And let him go to the treasurer for a rose-giulio[1] as the reward of dexterity. And then let him go to the master of the athletes, who hath order to take him in charge. And let the comptroller provide another tallow-scraper, who will do well not to waste Our tallow."

When the boy came down, the first tormentor disappointedly untied his wrists ; and, seizing them, hoisted him in the usual manner : while the other, having turned his garment over his head, scored *xij* criss-cross weals on his plunging hams with a cane.

Anon being released, the freshly sprouted athlete stifled his yells ; and he instantly stood on his head with his arms and legs spread as widely apart as possible.

Everybody burst out laughing.

There was commotion at the door of the audience-chamber.

Gioffredo woke up and would have been precipitate : for chamberlains were announcing :

---

[1] About a shilling, with four times its purchasing value.

"The Exalted Tranquillity of the Tyrant Lucrezia Borgia-Sforza of Pesaro."

Beating as quickly as possible then was the heart in my bosom, instantly sensing the coming of its mate in my maid's.

XVIII

ALL the women in the audience-chamber were
plebeian, ugly, stinking.   But this most beautiful princess brought in the odours of a garden
of fragrant herbs ; and, among the bevy attending her, I saw my maid.

Her eyelashes were lowered : but, every
now and then, she flashed a glance on this side
and on that, as though she were seeking something.   I knew what she was seeking.

But I shrank down in my corner, pulling
the impetuous Gioffredo with me : for I was
not conscious that the opportune moment had
arrived, even now.

The crowd opened a pathway for the tyrant.
A stool was set for her under the canopy near
Ippolito.   Her maids-of-honour stood behind
her.   All their hair was dyed yellow with oil
of honey in imitation of their mistress : but

my maid's hair was as black as a sapphire in a night without light.

The chamberlains emptied a great space in front of the dais, pressing back the crowd.

But I and Gioffredo thrust ourselves through, not to the front rank but to the second : for I did not wish to be seen, and I did wish to hear.

The tyrant thus addressed the cardinal, saying :

"We are come, o lord cardinal, from visiting Our mother. Madonna Giovannozza[1] rejoiceth by cause that the Keltic soldiers are departed : for she hath been in terror lest they should rob the blossoms of her orchard, the which is her heart's treasure ; and the revenues of her late husband's bequest suffice not for the pay of an armed guard. Wherefore, We are sworn to ask Our Most Blessed Father

---

[1] This was her nickname (Big Jenny), which she commonly bore in accordance with the Roman custom : but her real name was Giovanna de' Catanei.

for the immunity of her inn[1] against taxation and against the excise-duty on wines, so that she may reap a little profit in these hard times."

She spoke rapidly, as her young brother did, but in a voice which was very sweet and soft to hear. But it was clear to me that she had other more important things to say by side of this gossip. Ippolito also perceived it : for he sagaciously nodded his head, smiling in silence.

The tyrant continued, saying :

"Thou goest at noon to dine with Our Most Blessed Father, o Cardinal of Ferrara. His Blessedness is very lonely, very grave.

---

[1] The Lion Inn in Bear Street, a bequest from her deceased husband. Excepting perhaps the sixty Roman patricians, no one in those days thought a whit the worse of a lady for getting her living banaysically than people do now. Madonna de' Catanei was neither a barmaid nor a female boniface. She was the proprietor of the most celebrated hostelry in Rome ; and lived privately on her income in a villa near San Pietro ad Vincula.

He taketh hardly the defect of the Vice-chancellor, whom He hath loved much : for He cannot see that Sforza needs must stand by Sforza in these horrid quarrels. As for those Keltic invaders, He saith that the end is not yet: that, though they go now, anon they will return: that there will be war, perhaps during *iij* months, but not in the City: but that there first will be happenings which will astound the Christian King."

Ippolito appended grave nods and impenetrable smiles.

Madonna Lucrezia again tried to approach the matter which she had in mind, saying:

"After Lent, o lord cardinal, it is Our intention to dine daily in the gardens of La Magliana[1] to the sound of luths. Madonna Giulia[2] hath brought *iiij* luthists from Venice;

---

[1] A paparchal villa in the Campagna, ten miles S.E. of Rome, founded by Xystus the Fourth and enlarged by Innocent the Eighth, the predecessor of Alexander the Sixth.

[2] Giulia (Farnese) Orsini, a lady of the court.

and one is an improvisatore. We therefore beg that thou wilt be Our beadsman, giving Us the benefit of thine holy prayers for fair weather after Eastertide."

Ippolito conceded a gesture of assent. What was the use of a cardinal-deacon, excepting to pray for fair weather for fair ladies who were minded to dine in gardens, his aspect seemed to say. Having obtained so small a boon, the tyrant (womanlike) instantly demanded a great one, saying :

"And now, o Cardinal of Ferrara, We desire to hear thy news."

To whom he responded, saying :

"Since yesterday, divers strange things have happened. One of Our athletes, by race a Dacian, hath been murdered ; and his murderer even now is tolerating torment before strangulation."

Madonna Lucrezia interrupted, saying :

"The news which We desire are not of that nasty species."

Ippolito added :

o

" There are not any news of affairs known to Us, save those of Our family and those which Thine Exalted Tranquillity hath named."

Madonna Lucrezia looked him up and down. She would try the effect of a taunt ; and continued, saying :

" Our Most Blessed Father sitteth in the Castle of Santangelo, dumb, but smiling at His thoughts. Of what pleasant thing is He thinking ? There is not anyone in the City who will respond to Our inquiries. The others, perchance, cannot : but thou canst and wilt not, o Cardinal of Ferrara."

She was becoming indignant, but sorry. A dark woman never ought to inflame herself with anger, by cause that the black or the brown of her hair and the red of her rage are the colours of our old enemy, the devil : but fury augmenteth the beauty of a fair woman to the highest degree, for it brighteneth the clear blue of her eyes, while the poppy-colour of her face is exquisitely allied with the straw-colour of her hair. At such a moment, she resembleth a joyful field ready for reaping ; and happy is the youth who is bold enough to reap.

Ippolito was a little confused ; but he used himself serenely enough, saying that (for his part) he was willing but unable.

The tyrant no longer restrained her spleen. She spoke, while her fair cheeks flamed, scornfully saying :

"It is well known to Us that the Cardinal of Ferrara doth profess himself to be the friend of the Cardinal of Valencia. Our mind telleth Us also that the said Cesare is this day in some dire peril, having gone away with that very abominable Keltic king. Wherefore We should have thought that the Cardinal of Ferrara, having so many vigorous familiars in his hand, would be doing something for the safety of his friend. Or are all these mighty and magnificent gentlemen merely for show but not for use ?"

And then, o Prospero, my darling little maid burst out incontinent, saying :

"At least one of the Lord Cardinal's gentlemen is useful and willing as well as magnificent and mighty and very beautiful, o Exalted Tranquillity."

Everybody shouted with laughter at such effrontery. Her blushes burned her like a fire : but she maintained her situation bravely in front of the other girls ; and her eyes glittered like stars, blue-black, brilliantly beaming. I almost believed that she actually saw me : but I kept my face behind the head of a fool, peeping between his hood and the twisted liripipe of the same.

Madonna Lucrezia changed her posture, with the alacrity of one who findeth that her seat is a nest of scorpions, demanding shrilly, mockingly :

"What doth a maid-of-honour know about a cardinal's beautiful gentlemen ?"

There was a noise at the door ; and chamberlains entered announcing :

"The Exalted Potency of the Princess Sancia d'Aragon Borgia of Squillace."

I instantly cuddled Gioffredo's head as tightly as possible, pressing one wrist into his very wide-open mouth ; and, at the same time, despite my fast failing strength, with the other hand I seized him in a certain grip from which no one may move an hair's breadth. Nor did I release him without a promise of silence, asked in a whisper, granted by green eyes bulging and glaring. Thus we *ij* stood staring at the form of his wife.

XVIIII

SHE came in with her own galaxy of maids-of-honour, all in black habits, waving her hands and swaying her head distractedly, querulously blaming everybody.

She was a fat girl, very long in the back, red-haired, white-fleshed; and her eyes resembled those of a bereaved cow. A large nurse stepped closely behind her, carrying a baby swaddled on a board, terribly squealing. This, together with the recriminations now proceeding at the throne, and the occasional howls of the Princess of Squillace, and the shrieking laughter of the crowd, produced a tumult resembling that of Navona at Epiphany.[1]

Another stool having been set on the

---

[1] The Epiphany Fair in the Square of Navona, where everybody screeches and blows tin horns.

dais, the new comers arranged themselves in order.

Gioffredo's wife wept loudly until everyone was silent. Then she began to speak, saying :

"Ah-hoo, o Lord Cardinal, We are come for consolation, ah-hoo, ah-hoo, ah-he-he-he-he. For thou shalt know that Cesare hath gone to Naples ; and Our Fredo hath followed him, ah-hoo, ah-hoo, ah-he-he-he-he. We desire to know why. Ah-hoo. We desire to know why. Ah-he-he-he-he-hoo. Now we all will be compelled to sell our jewels. Now we all will be compelled to be ransomed, ah-hoo, ah-hoo. Why hath not Lucrezia prevented Cesare from going ? Why hath not this Purpled Person prevented Our Fredo from following ? Both those impetuous adolescents were in this very palace during the past night : for Fredo himself said so. And now he hath deserted Us, his most loving wife ; and hath ridden after Cesare with a mere handful of an escort, and on swift horses, ah-hoo. Three hours ago, We missed him. Four hours and who knoweth how much more, have We been a widow, and Our baby but a month old, a-hoo, a-hoo. Lord Cardinal, We desire Our husband. Ah-he-he-he-he-hoo. Hoo."

She tottered toward the large nurse; and set herself to moo over her baby, mumbling it with her lips from time to time. I wished for the death of the brat and its mother: for I feared that I should not be able to restrain Gioffredo much longer. That prince was wriggling like a clean dolphin.

Ippolito's visage showed the extreme discomfort of his mind.

The Tyrant Lucrezia spat out a sentence, saying:

" We are unable to treat such people with patience. Women do not become widows every time when their husbands run after the soldiers. Hath not Our Own husband gone to assist his cousin, Duke Lodovico Sforza-Visconti of Milan, and the Kelts,[1] some months ago, before these wars began? And is there

---

[1] The Sforza were siding with Gaul.

any Roman temerarious enough, or suburban enough, to denominate Alexander's daughter Widow on that count ?"

The Princess Sancia bewailed herself, saying that she wanted her Fredo.

But now indeed Gioffredo began to jump about, disturbing the people whose bodies had concealed us ; and I was totally unable to hold him. For, having broken away from me, he bounded towards his wife, very agitated, roaring like Stentor. And, at the same moment, Ippolito, catching a glimpse of me, emitted tremendous shouts of welcome, calling me by name.

But mine eyes were directed toward my maid. Now that this long (and, as I think, rather silly) period of concealment at length was concluded, I had no thoughts in my breast save of her who, unknowingly, had nerved me to my great exploit. Wherefore, there being no longer any cause for secrecy, I attempted to rush to her.

But it became clear that I could do no more

than limp, slowly, painfully, very ungracefully ; and, when *vij* paces had extricated me from the crowd, placing me alone in the empty space in the middle of the audience-chamber, where I instantly felt myself to be the target for the arrows of more than *dccc* eyes, then I suddenly remembered that my yellow-silver hair was knotted in an abominable night-cap, that the flesh of my body and limbs was a great deal more than half-naked, that I stank most indelicately, that I was besmirched and begrimed from head to foot with sweat and mire and every kind of uncleanness.

Such a terrific piece of knowledge caused me to utter yells, and to bolt (like a rabbit into his burrow) through the tapestried door at the side of the audience-chamber. Tumults of laughter pursued me ; and lent wings to my flight.

XX

Having made shift to get as far as the threshold of my proper antechamber, my limbs failed me there ; and I sank to the ground.

The way through the palace was long and devious. All the family was in the audience-chamber ; and I encountered no assistant on my painful passage.

I was so utterly exhausted that I ceased to care for anything at all ; and the mind in my breast advised me to lie still, until such time when my servitors should come to me. For, it being known that I had returned to the palace, I did not doubt but that search would be made for me.

That antechamber, o Prospero, was a very long room panelled with slabs of lapis-lazuli and malachite. The ceiling of it was painted with the images of the Divine Hylas struggling with the nymphs. I deliberated that my maid was fairer than any of these ; and I wondered what she might be doing at that moment.

The sunlight streamed in through the row of windows which abutted on the court, brightening the gilding of the cornice. On the other side all the outer doors of my divers chambers stood open ; but I continued to lie where I was on the very threshold of the antechamber, happy, drowsy, not anxious to go further.

Anon, a posse of my familiars came running up the stairs behind me, moaning and shouting commiseration for my condition : who, having carried me into the bathing-chamber, stripped me, and began to perform their office. And now indeed my mind devised new schemes ; and I became most anxious for instant restoration of my normal aspect. Wherefore, I condemned them for a parcel of fools and lazy oaves ; and I issued divers peremptory commandments.

Pages galloped hither and thither to and

from the wardrobe, bringing towels, ewers of various waters, and all the apparatus of washing, with numerous ceremonial garments, trays of jewels, flasks of the quintessence of southernwood, and the paraphernalia of mine estate.

While my flesh was being scrubbed, I selected a certain very singular new habit, which, by the benignance of my stars, I had caused to be made, when I first entered the City, for just such an occasion as the present appeared likely to be. For now my mind was persuaded that but one more turn of Divine Fortune's wheel would bring me to the top. But here my meditations were interrupted.

Ippolito with the Tyrant Lucrezia, and Gioffredo with the Princess Sancia, and mine own maid with all the company, came bounding up the stair inquiring for me.

A gesture from the chamberlains at my door kept them in the antechamber. The said door was not quite shut; and, having put my wet hair away from mine eyes, I was able (through the crevice) to see Gioffredo and his wife going to the embrasure of one of the windows. There they sat down, billing and cooing : but the others, unseen by me, began to bombard me with questions.

Ippolito vociferated, saying :

" Gioffredo saith that thou hast done that which thou didst set out to do. Tell us of the same, o Sideynes."

To whom I briefly responded (for, at the moment, the page on the stool was deluging me with hot water), saying :

" Pietrogorio hath received both messages ; and he desireth nothing better than to die for the Cardinal of Valencia, o Hebe."

But, when I had said this, I noted that my servitors were wearing a rather desperate aspect: nor durst they give more than deprecating gestures and sad imploring glances to my prompt interrogations. Wherefore, having commanded them to bring mirrors, I placed myself between the same in order that I might examine my person. What I saw on the flesh of my back caused me to utter certain very fervent objurgations.

The people in the antechamber with one voice instantly demanded the cause of mine anger.

To whom I indignantly responded, saying that the cyphers evidently were indelible : for vigorous scrubbing with hot water and lupin-meal only rendered my white flesh whiter, but the diagram itself remained clearly grey. It was a terrific predicament.

A certain page suggested an application of pumice : but I indignantly denied him, not being willing to have my smooth flesh roughened and ruined.

Those friends of mine in the antechamber cackled with laughter at my discomfiture ; and Madonna Lucrezia implored me to exhibit the accursed inscription. Ippolito also placed a similar request : to whose voice all the others added theirs.

My pages having swathed me in dry sheets

(covering me from head to foot like a shrouded cadaver but exposing my back), I placed myself for a few moments in the open doorway. Everybody giggled ; and came near. I heard their snuffling gasps of exclamation ; and felt the warm breath of the heads which stooped to gaze. No one was able to read the cyphers. These be they, o Prospero.

The Tyrant Lucrezia instantly averred that this was a lovely device for embroidering in gold on the front of a bodice, and that such a work would drive the plain Marchioness of Mantua mad with envy.

Ippolito, having traced the grey lines slowly with the tip of a loving finger (for so I felt it to be), stated an opinion that this was the kabbalistic character invented by Messer Honorios, formerly of Thebes, which Cesare was known to have taken from that erudite Gothic boy called Enrico Cornelio Agrippa von Nettesheim, who now is a councillor of the Emperor. In this case, he said, no one could read it save Cesare only and his proper familiars. As for the defilement of my flesh, he said, it no doubt would wear off in time.

And then I rejoiced very greatly : for I heard the dear little voice of my maid, saying :

" We will offer most fervent prayers that

the lord cardinal's prediction may not lack fulfilment."

At which words Madonna Lucrezia suddenly turned to examine the last speaker, instantly becoming agog for match-making. In her opinion, so she said, so beautiful a gentleman was fit to be anybody's husband.

Ippolito put in a salient word about the Great Ban.

That, she said, could not be permitted to run longer in despite of such an one as I had shown myself to be. For which cause, she said, the beautiful and blameless gentleman in the doorway instantly must hasten to the Castle of Santangelo with the present company, in order to tell all the tale to our Lord the Paparch Himself.

I howled with delight; and, having leaped forward into my secret chambers, I commanded the pages to indue me with mine habits using extreme celerity.

Ippolito cried out, inquiring whether Pietrogorio had read the cypher message to me,

demanding also what the said noble was going
to do.

To whom I responded, saying that His
Nobility had read the inscription as signifying :
"Statim adveniunt Gallicani, cum iis ego, obses
retentus : fac ut exquiras, et auxilium praestes
—The Gallicans are upon thee, with me as
their hostage ; find me, and lend succour : "
and the autograph, " C. Car^{al} de Valencia."
Also I said that I was ignorant of Pietrogorio's plans, knowing only that he had sent
me to buy up all the horses at the post-
house of Cinthyanum in Cesare's name. And
I added that the said adolescent, in my
judgment, was not only a very Odysseys
for deep-scheming, but also a gentleman with
whom it would be safe to play odd-and-even in
the dark.

Having pondered these words, Ippolito
began to have an inkling of Pietrogorio's
plan. So he said. For there are but *ij*
leagues between Velletri and Cinthyanum,
which last city doth belong to Rome ; and,

if Cesare could get there and find himself
master of all means of transit, he would have
no difficulty in effecting a speedy return.
But those *ij* leagues were the crux of the
affair.   Such was Ippolito's sentence.

The Tyrant Lucrezia delivered herself of
another opinion.   She said that Cesare was
a beast, a fine beast, an admirable beast, an
irresistible beast, and just now a necessary
(nay) an indispensable beast.   And she was
quite certain that he would contrive to cover
those *ij* leagues.

But, at the moment of speaking, at length
I escaped from my pages, radiant, delicate,
princely, in a habit of state.

XXI

I CAME out into the antechamber, very vivid, very vigorous, for fatigue seemed to have left my limbs, very pale and clean, for I was myself again, very grand - eyed, for lovely pleasant things were waiting for me to look upon them. My smooth hair was glittering like a cocoon, sunlit, delicate. My garb was shining silk, white as pearls, adorned with silver set with great cabochon moonstones. The armorials of mine house were emblazoned on my breast, not in our ordinary tinctures of white and red but in white and black, *videlicet* Luna and Saturn party per pale, a cross potent party per pale Saturn and Luna.[1]

---

[1] Really, this is just like Don Tarquinio's naive arrogance. Instead of being content with the ordinary nomenclature of his tinctures (Argent and Sable),

Everybody made haste to inspect me.

Ippolito said that he never had seen these habits before.

To whom I responded, saying that I had had them prepared secretly for the day when I should come face to face with our Lord the Paparch ; and that they bore a certain signification. I in fact had made myself as it were a book which His Sanctity might read. He would see youth and strength and ability : He would see the candid whiteness of innocence : He would see the blazon of mine house blackened by the Great Ban, whitening with the dawn of hope. But, having said these things, I became conscious of the eyes of my maid, a few paces away, gazing upon me with adoration : at whom I instantly precipitated myself, forgetting the others.

---

disdaining even the form used by peers (Pearl and Diamond), he needs must use the terms which are employed only in blazoning the armorials of a sovereign ! Certainly his lineage has no equal in this world. But——! Well——! There——!

Madonna Lucrezia put in a sentence, saying :

"All these things are very poetic and pretty ; and the beautiful and blameless gentleman certainly is most urbane : but We take pride in Ourself by cause that We are purely practical.   Furthermore, all the damage, which is done on this orb of earth, is done either by saying the right things to the wrong person, or the wrong things to the right person.   These admirable words ought not to be uttered to Us, but to Our Most Blessed Father.   Wherefore, the present company instantly must go to the Castle of Santangelo.   Boy !   Litters ! At the Vatican, a division shall be made, not to embarrass Our Most Blessed Father with a show of force.   The Cardinal of Ferrara hath the right of demanding a boon, by cause that he provided the swift runner.   The beautiful and blameless gentleman hath an equal right, by cause that he ran swiftly.   Let those *ij* demand their said boons.   If they win them, well.   In any case, after dinner, when Our

Most Blessed Father is in a good humour and will concede anything for the sake of being left to His afternoon nap, then We Ourself and Our well-beloved brother, Don Gioffredo, will enter The Presence prepared to intercede. But the Lord Alexander is just and gentle; and He will be propitious. Litters! Boy! Litters!"

Half a score of pages fled down the stair with Her Tranquillity's commandments. No one said any more: for there was nothing more to be said. Our several families began to collect themselves, while we washed our fingers; and anon we left the antechamber in due order.

In the courtyard, the tyrant and the princess and their maids ascended the litters: but we others took horse in full state; and so we set forth, a very grand procession, but not unusual in those old days, o my parthenean Prospero, when a pageant of princes going to pay respects to the Pontifex Maximus was common enough.

We went by Lungara. I rode by side of
Ippolito. We both were silent, pondering the
matter in hand.

As we passed the great Riarj Palace on the
left, where the white-faced cardinal was entertaining The Beloved,[1] I said :

"They say that one liveth there who
knoweth more Greek than We do."

It was a silly irrelevant word, uttered only
by cause that I did not wish to seem either
sulky or afraid. Ippolito shook his head,
soberly saying :

"No one knoweth more Greek than thou,
o Sideynes."

Thereafter we rode without speaking. I
knew that I was as nervous as a February
sparrow, jipping and flirting, and liable to
twitter entirely automatically. For which cause

---

[1] This would be that very wonderful person of
Rotterdam called Gerard, who (having no legal surname)
translated his Flemish Christian name (which means
"The Beloved") into its Latin and Greek equivalents,
Desiderius Ἐρασμιος, by which combination indeed we
know him now as Desiderius Erasmus.

I set myself to consider who I was, and what I had done, and how extremely notable mine aspect was. I contemplated myself, my mind, my body, my qualities, capabilities, exploits, desires. I also called to remembrance the benignance of my stars. And behold it was all very good. So we came to Vatican.

Nothing disturbed me. Nothing ever again would disturb me. Was I not riding in triumph, to the Giver of Bays?

XXII

HAVING parted from our companions and dismissed our trains, I and Ippolito walked along the high gallery, emerging at length on the vast corridor of the castle, spiral, gloomy. Below were labyrinthine depths. We ascended several little stairs, passing through numerous antechambers hung with porphyry-coloured arras. The odour of the place was sepulchral.

A ruffled flunkey in a Spanish habit of black, with cloak and sword, drew aside a thick porphyry-coloured curtain; and we passed out of darkness into the blazing sunlight of The Presence.

We were on a secluded terrace on the summit of the fortress. Beyond the battlements, we could see the panorama of all Rome and the Campagna with the Alban

Mount on the distant horizon. Tiber seemed to be a chain of chrysoliths meandering among mounds of emeralds. So lofty a situation was convenient for Him, Whose authority was world-wide.

Some orange-trees in tubs formed a screen in the shadow of a turret. A square carpet, porphyry-coloured, was spread on the pavement. A throne-like chair, raised on one step, with a foot-stool and cushions and other stools, all of the same colour, stood upon it.

Here sat the Ruler of the world, the Father of princes and kings, the earthly Vicar of Jesus Christ our Saviour, the Paparch Alexander, magnificent, invincible, alone and reading in His breviary.

I will tell thee, o Prospero, how that incomparable prince and pontiff appeared to me. He was habited in the white cassock, sash, and hosen, the porphyry-coloured shoes embroidered with gold crosses, the cape and cap of porphyry-coloured velvet, reversed with ermine, the golden paparchal stole.

The pallium of universal jurisdiction, well-woven, snow-like, was fixed, on His breast and shoulders, by diamond pins of the form of crosses potent elongate. A gold chain surrounded His neck ; and its pendent cross decorously was hidden in the folds of His cape.[1] The grand gold signet of the paparchy glittered on the first finger, and an enormous amethyst on the third of His right hand. He was in the sixty-fifth year of His age, of a robust habit of body ; and genial generous majesty distinguished the splendour of His Spanish features.

The chamberlains and pages in porphyry-coloured liveries, who stood about the turret-doorway, performed their genuflections ; and retired backward.

Ippolito let his great-cloak of ermine and vermilion fall to trail voluminously behind him ; and led me forward by the hand. I suddenly became conscious that I was very young

---

[1] This seems to be less ostentatious than the modern prelatic method.

and very slim by side of all this sumptuous
grandeur. I felt as a new taper feeleth when
stuck suddenly on high upon a pricket, rather
pleased with the light on its head: but
knowing that a mere flip of the finger can
break its body in twain and consign it to
the darkness of oblivion. But yet, remembering how diaphanously white and vivid
were mine aspect and my gait, I comforted
myself a little.

We kneeled at the foot-stool. Ippolito
kissed the paparchal hand: I, the cross on
the shoe.

The Archiereys closed His prayer-book,
looking with inquiry from me to Ippolito,
and back again to me. I perceived admiration in His glance which swept and enveloped
me; and I knew that my stars were benignant.
I was glad.

Ippolito stood up: but I remained on
my knees. He took mine hand; and presented me by name, reciting my style and
estate.

Our Lord the Paparch did not remove his glance from me: nor I, mine from Him.

Ippolito continued his discourse, stating mine abominable condition, naming my natural abilities as well as the disabilities which, as a bandit, I was compelled to tolerate ; and he briefly narrated the deed which I had done, meriting favour. And at length he made an end.

Our Lord the Paparch gave me a sign to rise, saying nothing. I alertly sprang to my feet ; and took *ij* paces backward, from the shadow into the full glare of the sun, stiffening my strong knees, standing well-poised and very rigidly erect indeed. So, having shaken mine hair from mine eyes, I looked squarely and superbly in the face of His Sanctity.

He intently regarded me during *ij* or *iij* moments. Then He said :

" Let Us hear thy voice, that We may know thee."

I drew in a very long breath, inflating my breast, raising my head and shoulders ; and began to speak, gravely, slowly, saying that I knew myself to be in the presence of the Ruler of the world, Whose plenitude of power could reinstate mine house of Poplicola di Hagiostayros, no one contradicting, or could eradicate the same utterly by means of the Great Ban—power, I said, of making or of marring.

Then I hesitated : for sudden overwhelming conviction of mine helpless insignificance rushed into my mind. I poured out a torrent of words. What was I, I said, in the sight of the Father of princes and kings, but a negligible worm.

And impotent fury, at my total dependence on the Paparch's will and pleasure, inflamed me. My face tingled with angry blood, at the thought that anyone should be my superior, at the knowledge that I knew myself to be this One's inferior and had confessed the same. But instantly, with a very vehement effort, I mastered mine emotions ; and continued speaking, deliberately, even frigidly, while the bowels terrifically throbbed within my body. I said :

"But I will not sue. There are no crimes on my soul which are matter for pardon. I will not ask for favour. But, rather than live another hour, blameless under the Great Ban which I have not merited, I will dive headlong from these near battlements, that the candour of mine innocence may shatter the blood-stained stones of Rome."

Thus having spoken, I flashed mine eyes to the side for an instant, noting the place whence I would spring. Then I looked back with most fierce determination, alert and ready to leap before Ippolito could lay his mighty hands on me, standing intense, expecting paparchal fulminations.

Our Lord the Paparch eyed me up and down, comprehending each plane and contour of the incarnate independence, pallid, not uncomely in defiance, which refused to ask for right as a grace. And anon He very gently said :

Q

"Dear lovely child, think not so unkindly of thy Father."

At those words, sublime, benignant, my throat was constricted and my knees trembled very exceedingly. Mine eyes glared upon the Paparch and the cardinal in turn, without seeing either of those personages. Then I looked upward to the empyrean where the gods live: for surely it was a god's voice which I had heard; and I noted a little sky-lark soaring above me, singing like an angel. Nothing else was visible to me at that moment. My body was simply tottering by cause of the sudden violent evanescence of my fury.

I sank on my knees, very meekly kissing the extended hand of my Father.

The bells in all the turrets of the City began clanging in the new manner. It was the hour of noon.

Our Lord the Paparch and the Cardinal of Ferrara kneeled where they were; and said the prayers, Angelus Domini and the rest.

I also was kneeling, thankful enough for the interval granted while I conquered my weakness, recollecting myself.

XXIII

A COMPANY of paparchal familiars entered.
Some brought a table sustaining the apparatus
for dining. Others brought another table
covered with a fair linen cloth. On the last,
the cook placed a covered dish: the butler,
a dish of raisins and a basket of bread: the
cellarer, a glass flask of wine and another of
water. I never have seen a service so extremely
plain.

Being now fulfilled with vigour and thank-
fulness, I longed to do something dynamic.
Wherefore, I violently hustled three pages,
robbing them of the basin and the ewer and
the towel; and, on my knees, I did boy's
service, while our Lord the Paparch first
washed His hands.

He smiled at mine ardour: but knowing
(in His enormous wisdom) that I was excited

beyond measure, He addressed His words to Ippolito, saying:

"Most of thy colleagues, o Cardinal of Ferrara, are either in prison or in rebellion; and the orators[1] and the barons are unwilling to dine with Us, by cause that We so far abstain from carnal lusts in that a single dish sufficeth for our table. Consequently, when We find in Our hand, at dinner time, a cardinal-prince and a Roman patrician, it is but natural that they should become Our guests. What is enough for one is enough for *ij*, and what is enough for *ij* is enough for *iij*. Let then stools be set for the cardinal and for this white flame of adolescence."

So this Sanctity deigned to give order.

The table, being an high one, was wheeled to our Lord the Paparch where He sat on His elevated chair. But our stools were heightened

---

[1] The ambassadors of the Powers, who, at this epoch, did most of their ambassadorial business in flowery rhetoric.

by cushions. Very strange ceremonial was observed at this meal.

A chamberlain presented a bundle of napkins, from which we each selected *ij*. With the first, we scrupulously rubbed our platters and knives and forks and moss-agate cups, before using the same. With the second, we protected our garments from slops, or wiped our mouths before drinking. All this being strange to me, I carefully imitated the example of Ippolito, perceiving him to be acquainted with the practice. But I wondered greatly what might be the significance of such elaborate functions. And anon it was given to me to understand.

For the cook, having uncovered the dish, genuflected ; and presented beef and olives to Our Lord the Paparch : Who Himself deigned to cut off a mouthful at random, putting the same on a fork with an olive similarly selected ; and watched the said cook eating both morsels. This having been done, His Sanctity took His portion of the viands ;

and the dish was brought to us others in
turn.   In like manner, the butler proffered
the bread-basket ; and ate crust and crumb of
the Paparch's choosing, before any bread was
so much as touched by us *iij*.   The same
ceremony having been kept with the raisins,
the dish and the basket were established
on the table under our eyes.   The cellarer
brought also the wine and water ; and, having
drunk a cupful of both, which the Paparch
deigned to pour for him, he filled for us, and
placed the flasks by side of the dish of
raisins.

By this time, I had become conscious that
these practices merely were a substitute for the
customary venom-taster ; and, all incontinent,
I said, by way of comment, that life would
not be worth my while, if I were compelled
to take so many meticulous precautions against
venom every time when I desired to satiate
mine hunger.

Our Lord the Paparch retorted on me,
saying :

"The life of Him who is God's Vicegerent is not worth any man's while."

And He began to speak to Ippolito, as soon as the servitors had left us alone, questioning him very acutely concerning the events of the night and morning. It was very strange to hear Him talking of the Cardinal of Valencia :[1] for He by no means spoke of that splendid purpled person, tawny, tiger-like, as a father speaketh of the son of his loins, nor did He speak of the said adolescent as a slave speaketh of his tyrant or as a victim speaketh of his persecutor, in despite of those who very vainly have alleged that Cesare dominated the indomitable Alexander : but it seemed to me that He spoke of him rather as one would speak of a servant of hyperexcellent parts, whom one employeth for

[1] This piece of the holograph, although not exactly germane to the thread of the story (except in so far as it is the reflections of Don Tarquinio while a guest at the paparchal dinner-table), is extremely interesting as history, especially to all sorts of silly daws who would like to try to pretend to think otherwise.

the sake of another who is served by such employment of such a servant. And this indeed is true : for we now know that Madonna Giovannozza bore Cesare to Giuliano[1] before she bore Juan Francisco[2] and Lucrezia and Gioffredo to Rodrigo ;[3] and, that Alexander should have deigned to advance the fortunes of Cesare, as well for that splendid prince's own utility as for the love which He bore for the mother of the same, is only natural. But, while I was excogitating the matter, I did not omit to devour as much food as decorum permitted, I being most terrifically hungry, and the attention of the other *ij* being diverted from me during nearly all the time.

And anon, at the end, our Lord the

---

[1] Cardinal Dellarovere (who afterward became Julius the Second) was named Giuliano.

[2] The young Duke of Gandia who was murdered.

[3] Cardinal Borja y Borja (who became Alexander the Sixth) was named Rodrigo. And here we seem to have gotten to the bottom of one of the many Borgia mysteries—viz., the real parentage and status of Cesare (called) Borgia.

Paparch thus addressed me by the same appellation as before ; and He used the Roman tongue in a very archaic manner, saying :

" Dear lovely child, what wouldst thou have and what canst thou do?"

But, before that I was able to utter a syllable, Ippolito interrupted, reciting a category of my numerous peculiar excellencies, which I will not include in this history, seeing that they are known to every man. But, after many words concerning my bravery, he ended with the assertion of Messer Pierettore that I could write Greek and speak it like Saint Gabriel Archangel.

This seemed to be intended as an advice to me : for which cause, seeing that the Paparch's grand eyes still dwelled on me as though expecting mine own response, I began to orate in the crisp and dulcet syllabification of Hellas, saying :

" Wisdom, as I suppose, is a different thing from courage."[1]

---

[1] χωρις δηπου σοφια εστιν ανδριας (Platōn).

But there our Lord the Paparch stopped me, saying again:

"Dear lovely child, thou shalt know that an old man like Ourself, Who hath been worried by recalcitrant kings and by other naughty men, hath forgotten all the Greek which He ever knew, save the wail of that scribe who wrote, Would that We could grow young again."[1]

But the saying was a pathetic one, tear-bringing, love-inspiring; and, at that moment, I could not think of anything better to say than that I was in all things obedient to His sovereign will.

He was listening very intently: for, having afforded me so much time for recollection, I think that He expected me to make an elaborate discourse. But I, being mindful of His supremacy not less than of His generosity, preferred to show an equal generosity and confidence on mine own part: for which cause,

[1] ἀνηβητηριαν ῥωμην ἐπαινω λαμβανειν (Eyripides).

I responded as aforesaid. He urged me then to make a formal definite petition: but, being indeed very pleased with the form of words which I had used, I continued to respond to all His urging, saying only:

"I am in all things obedient to my sovereign's will."

At this the paparchal pages returned, bringing the rosewater for our last hand-washing. This duty having been performed and the psalm ended, they removed the tables and retired.

Ippolito stood up, stretching his gigantic limbs and combing his hair: but our Lord the Paparch was observing me all the time. As the servitors were going away, He shot a sudden commandment after them to bring a skin of parchment, with ink and pens and pounce.

This having been done, and we *iij* being alone again, He ordained that I should bring my stool near to Him, having thrown the cushions aside, and having placed the writing materials on it; and also that I should kneel there, ready to write.

Thus, He Himself dictated to me the petition, which thou, o Prospero, knowest to be the most precious document in thy father's archives. But, although thou hast seen the same so often that its contents are impressed indelibly on thy memory, nevertheless I will not omit to transcribe it here, in order that this history may be perfect and complete, *videlicet:*

The petition of the Roman patrician named Tarquinio Giorgio Drakontoletes Poplicola di Hagiostayros
is
that he may be delivered from the Great Ban,
that he may be relieved from all disabilities,
that he may be absolved from all canonical censures and excommunications,
in his own person,
and
in the persons of all of his house:

also

that he himself may be named among the Advo-
      cates of the Sacred Consistory, where he
      may use his mind :

also

that he himself may be named among Our knights
      of Saint George for the Defence of Christen-
      dom, where he may use his body against
      the foes of our Most Holy Faith.

Thus He spoke and thus I had written :
but when I conned it over, as I threw the
golden pounce upon the wet ink, a kind of
terror seized me ; and I began again to shake
like one in a palsy. And suddenly a new
diversion occurred.

Numerous footsteps and voices approached
the door of the turret, wafting a delicate odour
as of women and love.

XXIIII

Madonna Lucrezia entered with her galaxy of maids, who did obeisance ; and crossed the terrace toward the battlements. There they stood, admiring the view, moving a little among themselves like flowers in a breeze. But the tyrant came and sat on one of the cushions near the Paparch's footstool, between me and Ippolito, facing us both.

She put a most delicate hand on the archieratic knee ; and thus she spoke, saying :

"Dear and Most Holy Father, I hope that Thou hast been doing justice to this beautiful and blameless gentleman."

But, while she was speaking, yet more noises came from the door of the turret ; and Gioffredo entered with his wife and their baby and their several trains. The prince and princess seated themselves on the other cushions on the step of the throne: but their familiars drifted away to the other maids-of-honour who were already by the battlements.

I was kneeling still with the portentous parchment under mine hand. All my body was quaking terribly: for I was not quite able to believe in my good fortune, and rather feared that I was being played with.

Ippolito, having drawn up a stool, sat by my side in front of the Paparch and His children.

I durst not move from my knees: but I cast a quick look among the maids for my proper maid. She instantly caught it, returning a smile, very lovely, soul-inspiring. Wherefore I comforted myself, knowing that my stars most certainly were benignant.

But Madonna Lucrezia and her brother began to make intercession on mine account; and Ippolito joined himself to them from time to time. The *iij* voices blended very harmoniously, *videlicet*, the clear treble of the girl, the counter-tenor of the boy as insistent and mellow as a bell, the bass of the young cardinal, sonorous, profound.

I at first listened very gratefully to their melodious intonation : but anon, the things which they said of me afflicted me with nausea. I have done many great and noble deeds, with my body as well as with mine intellect ; and I am not ashamed of esteeming the same according to their merits, or of hearing them praised in convenient terms. But enough is as good as a feast ; and at this moment I had heard enough and more than enough. Wherefore, with mine eyes I strove most earnestly, imploring Ippolito and Gioffredo to be favourable to their tongues. All to no purpose. They continued to speak ; and I perforce was compelled to kneel where I was, listening, blushing with augmenting fury.

At length our Lord the Paparch signed for silence ; and He said :

" We have heard you, o lord cardinal and

R

o dearest daughter and o dearest son ; and We thank you for your good offices. But intercessors are not necessary in this present matter: for Our dear lovely child here present hath an exceedingly definite notion of what is due from Us to him ; and he hath set down the same most eloquently in writing."

And, having thus spoken, He took the parchment from me ; and handed it to the others.

Ippolito already had heard what I had written by commandment: but Madonna Lucrezia and Gioffredo put their heads together, eagerly perusing the writing.

But the fine features of Alexander remained as imperscrutable as those of the sphynx.

His daughter looked at Him, trying to read the intention of His mind: but, having failed, she said:

"The beautiful and blameless gentleman hath merited these rewards at least ; and there is another reward known to me which he in any case shall have. But first deign a stroke of the pen here, o dear and Most Holy Father."

Thus she spoke: but we all suddenly began to hear very joyful shouts from the distance far below, surging nearer and nearer, ever augmenting. Crowds of familiars, baronial, cardinalitial, paparchal, came tumbling into The Presence, all phrenetically roaring.

But, while we stood and kneeled staring in amazement, the splendid Cardinal of Valencia also strode on to the terrace, panting, sweating, mud-stained, but elate with triumph. He wore an astonishing Neapolitan habit of green velvet, pinked and escalloped and purfled with orange-coloured satin, the same which I myself already had seen on another person in another city on that very day. His hosen were striped in green and orange-colour. His boots were of orange-coloured leather. His high conical green hat, long-peaked in front, was adorned by a tall orange-coloured feather: but his tawny hair bulged behind in a net of green cord. I never have seen a cardinal in such an incommodious guise before or since. And he dragged with him by the hand that noble Pietrogorio, of whom I already have written, who wore the vermilion habit which Cesare had worn when he left us during the night, which habit now was very gravely disordered. Had it not been for their different voices, it would have been difficult to say which was the cardinal and which the noble : but, as it was, they only resembled twins in trouble, horribly dirty, tattered, dilapidated.

Gioffredo made himself heard in a sentence, saying that it would occupy the servitors of these gentlemen during *iiij* hours to correct the condition of their persons.

They fell on their kness ; and the Cardinal of Valencia began to bellow a narration of his adventures.

But our Lord the Paparch with a gesture produced silence. And anon He beckoned me to hold up my stool and to give Him the pen. This I did, holding my face low : in order to avoid the pricking of the multitudinous eyes which were impinging upon every bare part of my flesh. And, having taken the parchment, and having placed it on the stool, He began to write in this way, saying each word aloud as He wrote it ; and thus He said:

"It pleaseth Us, and so by Our Own impulse We command : Alexander the Sixth, Supreme Pontiff."[1]

And he gave the signed parchment into my tingling hands.

Having bent down to kiss the cross on His shoe, purely grateful, and having made obeisance to Madonna Lucrezia and to Gioffredo, and having embraced Ippolito, oblivious of manners I launched myself toward my maid by the battlements.

The moment was opportune. Everybody was approaching The Presence to hear the newest news: for mine affairs were no longer important. Could I have done aught else,

---

[1] Placet ; et ita, motu Proprio, Mandamus. Alexander VI P.M.

o Prospero? We were alone, at the back of the crowd. I offered to her the parchment, and my body and soul with it, kneeling on both my knees as one who kneeleth before some Divine One. But she raised me with a most gentle movement, giving herself all to me.

I cannot remember what happened in the in-suing minutes: but, when I once more became conscious of my circumstances, the Cardinal of Valencia, unchecked, was bellowing like the Borgia bull. I will set down the few words which I heard him saying: not that I paid much observance to him, for who, having the desire of his heart in his heart and pressed against his heart, would listen to another roaring of other matters? Yet, by cause of that cardinal's vociferations (and his teeth and his eyes gleamed the while like a tiger's, delicate, very triumphant in vigour), I could not avoid seeing his gestures and hearing the noise which he was making. He said:

"Having secluded me as aforesaid, this

Nobility changeth clothes with me; and forthwith betaketh himself in my room to the neighbourhood of the Keltic monkey. But I made haste to ride back to Cinthyanum, where during *iij* hours I waited in the house of which some of ye pretend to know. Anon, this Nobility cometh, laughing as though his cheeks were another's. For the Christian King, on preparing to ride from Velletri, quickly perceived that his hostage no longer was the Cardinal of Valencia; and, falling in a fume lest I myself should harass his rear, resolved to make a sudden dash for Naples, where he might fortify his camp. But he left behind him the Cardinal of Amboise and the Sieur de Commines, ordaining that they should strangle very worthy Nobility and fire his city. They did neither, admiring his courage and fidelity as much as I do— Pietrogorio, thou art Our locumtenens and signifer from to-day :—but, having put him near a fresh horse, they turned their backs and looked for him elsewhere, quietly evacu-

ating Velletri and following their master.
Wherefore this Nobility, seeing that his
escape was permitted, came to Cinthyanum,
and thence with me hither with all speed."

Thus he spoke. But Madonna Lucrezia,
not being overmuch entertained by his narration, was letting her sweet eyes rove round
among the company. And here she pointed
a mischievous finger at me and my maid:
for, at the moment, we by chance were lip to
lip. The crowd divided, exhibiting us in
that situation.

We instantly became conscious of a very
terrific silence, and of innumerable glances
stabbing us. Having recognised our predicament, we drew a little apart. Slight
giggles arising from the crowd, and the
glittering of innumerable teeth manifested
by innumerable smiles, further disconcerted
and dismayed us. We ran forward hand in
hand, kneeling before our Lord the Paparch.
I was hot with blushes: but I contrived to
stammer a few words, saying:

"Immense happiness is our excuse for indecorum in the Apostolic Presence: for, o Sanctity, we love one another."

Alexander, magnificent, invincible, benignly smiled upon us; and He deigned a response, saying:

"Love one another, o dear lovely children; and We will consecrate your love."

And He held out His hand for a ring.

Seeing how I was in the Paparch's favour, everybody instantly proffered all their rings. We might have been married with Ippolito's cardinalitial sapphire. Madonna Lucrezia offered *ij* handfuls. Prince Gioffredo thrust upon me his great table ruby. I might have had a peck-measure full of rings. But I myself was drawing off mine own jasper with the Scorpion and Ares,[1] being desirous of communicating the benignance of my stars with my maid, when the Cardinal of Valencia produced the enormous gilt-bronze ring, the cre-

---

[1] This appears to have been his nativity-ring, a jasper intagliate with ♏ and ♂.

dentials which had procured for him the swift runner. And we all realized the suitability of that.

Gioffredo, having brought the little silver stoup of holy water from the inside of the door of the turret, placed himself as acolyth at the right hand of his Most Holy Father.

The sky above our heads had the beautiful blue of spring-time, clear as the light in my maid's eyes. We were kneeling together in the freshness, high over the City and the world.

Out of profound silence, the strong voice of the Archiereys came to me, demanding whether I willed to have Hersilia as my wedded wife. To Whom I responded, saying :

" I so will have her."

He demanded of her whether she willed to have me as her wedded husband. To Whom she responded, saying :

" An it so please Thee, o Sanctity."

Everybody was smiling again. Our Lord the Paparch joined our hands. Having sprinkled the enormous ring and blessed it, He deigned it to me. I put it on the first, the second, and left it on the third left finger of my maid, saying the accustomed words which bound her indissolubly to me.

Our Lord the Paparch rose. All the company kneeled round us. Lifting His hand, He imparted Apostolic Benediction.

So He withdrew to His afternoon nap, like the life-giving sun, who sinketh, glorious, golden, to his rest in the sea.

XXV

Instantly, the light of The Presence having been extinguished, we were (so to speak) all in the dark.

Great confabulations insued. Everybody exuded important but perfectly preposterous propositions.

The Cardinal of Valencia was for raising armies wherewith to pursue the Keltic scamps; and put himself to speak seriously to the Cardinal of Este, inquiring how many mercenaries could be bought from Ferrara. But Ippolito would not have anything to say to him; and he went off, muttering, with his new lieutenant and standard-bearer.

But all the others came to converse with me. From what was said, certain matters appeared, which gave food for thought.

The question of my next act was discussed.

It seemed not to be decorous that I should live with my wife in the palace of the Cardinal of Ferrara. It clearly was my bounden duty to send news, of the removal of the Great Ban, to my cousin and our baron Marcantonio. I also desired very strenuously to go at once to my castle of Deira by the southern sea, there to arrange the transit of my goods and my familiars to the City, where I was intending to pass my life. Furthermore, I was famishing with hunger, not only for my maid but also for a meal, solid, interminable, seeing that I had been fasting since supper-time: for what I had eaten at the Paparch's table was no more than a snack.

Wherefore, the Cardinal of Valencia having disappeared, while the tyrant and the princess and their girls were chattering to my blushing wife (whose dear little hand I did not relinquish for a moment), I turned the other way; and, at length, contrived to overcome the loud voices of Ippolito and Gioffredo, proclaiming to them my necessities.

But, though they demurred from my departure, nevertheless they confessed that I spoke reasonably ; and, finally, after many words, Gioffredo offered an immediate banquet with lodgings at Traspontina till the evening, and Ippolito offered an escort of *xl* athletes and *xl* men-at-arms for our journey to Deira.

And anon we went to Traspontina. There we feasted. There we played. There we also slept. What we ate and drank, or what we did, in those *iiij* hours, I am unable to specify. For I was in a species of delirium, having no more mind and body than sufficed for these *ij* things, *videlicet* my wife, and mine insuing progress to the cradle of my race, in comparison with which all other worldly matters seemed very rightly to be of no price.

But at one hour before avemmaria, my valises having been brought from the Estense Palace and my wife's from the Apostolic Palace of Vatican, *viij* decurions of Ippolito's came with my proper *iij*, being a company of *cxxj* persons in all to attend us; and so we rode out from the City, on the first stage toward the eastern road which leadeth at length to Deira, in the cool of the evening

Thus, thy loving father hath set down the full history of the four-and-twenty hours of his fortunate day, not concealing anything which his own senses perceived; and he saith, that this is the manner in which history ought to be written, o Prospero, my son.

FELICITER